THE ONLY RED STAR I LIKED WAS A STARFISH

I0554500

ARMANDO SIMON

Published by Lulu Publishers
Morrisville, North Carolina

ISBN 978-0-615-23562-2

This book is dedicated to my daughter, Amanda, and my son, Apolo, in the hopes that the only red star that will ever hang over their heads will be Aldebaran.

And if it is a despot you would dethrone, see first that his throne erected within you is destroyed.

Kahlil Gibran, *The Prophet*

TABLE OF CONTENTS

JONAS SALK

There was a long, long line at the health clinic. Parents had brought their children to be vaccinated with the new, first ever, poliomyelitis vaccine. Some children played or talked with others whom either they had known beforehand or had just met, some watched them play with a curious mixture of shyness and longing to join them and others stayed close to their parents, either because they were shy or because their parents wouldn't let them play with the other children with a sudden irrational fear that, at the last second, their child would be stricken with polio by coming into contact with the other children seeking a polio vaccine, although just that morning their child had been playing in their neighborhood with other children. Overall, there was such a festive mood that even overlapped the kids occasionally remembering that needles would be used.

For months they had waited for the shipment of this new miracle vaccine, created by an American doctor with the name of Jonas Salk. His name was on *everyone's* lips, all over the world, on a daily basis, in newspapers, in newsreels at the movie theaters, in television, as frequently named as any famous politician or movie star. It was on several persons' lips while they waited in line. Even the children knew his name.

"If that man doesn't get the Nobel Prize, then there's no justice in this world."

"Ach, what a thing to say! Of course, they'll give him the Nobel Prize!"

"I read in the newspapers that he was getting mail from parents with money inside. Imagine! In appreciation!"

It was true. For many years---no, decades!---parents had seen pictures of little children with leg braces, children with half of their bodies paralyzed and in wheelchairs, even children condemned to live out their lives caged in an iron lung with only their little heads sticking out, pictures that would tear at the most hardened heart and every father, mother, grandparents, worldwide, would close their eyes in a shudder. For some perverse reason, the poliomyelitis vector had a predilection for children's nervous systems, though adults were occasionally stricken as well. Rumor had it that public drinking fountains were its favorite breeding ground and parents could often be heard yelling at their children not to drink from a public fountain at the parks, zoos, or other places.

Little by little, the line moved forward. One by one, the children were vaccinated. Adults could come back in a few months for theirs. The demand for the vaccine was overwhelming, not just in Cuba, but in each and every country and the makers were working around the clock. Everyone had the irrational, but unshakable, fear that *their* child would be struck with paralysis at the last minute while waiting for the vaccine to arrive, just as some soldiers towards the end of a war become overwhelmed with anxiety trying to avoid being killed by the last bullet fired at the last hour of the war.

Once vaccinated, the parents felt greatly relieved and full of gratitude for this Doctor Jonas Salk. The children felt pride in having participated in an important event and when asked, would proudly show the site of vaccination, deny having cried on being pricked, and would recite the names Jonas Salk with as much pride as they would recite the names Antonio Maceo or José Martí.

Ten years later, most people did not remember, or recognize, the name of Jonas Salk. Not in Cuba. Not in Thailand. Not in Egypt. Neither in Brazil, Norway, Italy, or Japan.

Not even in America.

And, a couple of decades later, in 1995, when Jonas Salk died, none of the news agencies, news magazine, or television news carried the news. But . . . as luck would have it, someone else died about just the same time and *he* was in the cover of news magazines. The journalists of newspapers, news magazines and television news gave long, detailed accounts of his life and cried out what a great loss to humanity his death had been. Jerry García, a barely literate drug addict and rock start had kicked the bucket.

JULIO

"Let's drop by the Ugalde's," Doctor Menendez told his wife.

"All right. It's a pretty day to go out," she agreed. "Wilfredito! Get ready to go out!" she yelled out.

"Where are we going, Mom?" he asked, coming towards her.

"To Ugalde's. You can play with Julio there."

Wilfredo, on hearing this, blanched and bolted back to his room and crept under his bed in fear.

He listened nervously as his parents got ready to go, hoping that they would go off without him, knowing that they would not, knowing that he would be forced to go along, knowing that he would have to be with Julio.

Doctor Menendez had treated Senor Ugalde for a heart condition and was now a regular patient. In Cuba, this automatically meant a concomitant personal relationship as well and this had resulted in a standing invitation for Doctor Menendez and his family to visit Ugalde at his mansion any time (also, in Cuba, you did not phone ahead in consideration to the other person, you just dropped in and they, in turn, were expected to drop whatever plans they had for that day). The Menendez enjoyed rubbing noses with the Ugaldes, who were rich. Wilfredo, their small son, did not.

"Wilfredito, are you ready? Where are you?" his mother asked. He stayed quiet.

"Now, where is he? Did he go out?"

One of the advantages to being a small child is that adults' perspectives are always taller, so you can hide things where they are less likely to look for, including yourself.

Now, he could hear them yelling his name out into the street in the offhand chance that he had gone out to play. Now, he heard them searching for him inside the house, their irritation evident in their voice and this, in turn, worried him. Finally, his father looked under his bed.

"What are you doing down there? Haven't you heard us calling you?"

"I'm not going! I don't want to go!"

"Come on out of there right now! What's wrong with you?"

Wilfredo emerged, sullen and scared that he might get whipped. His mother looked him over.

"Look at you, you aren't even dressed properly for a visit," she said and began to dress him hurriedly.

'I don't wanna go there."

"Why not? You always have fun there, you get to play with Julio."

"I don't like him, he always hurts me. Always!"

"Tch! What nonsense you talk!"

"Can't you drop me over at grandma's house?"

"No, it's on the other side of town from where we're going."

"But, I don't want to go to Julio's house!"

"OK, you're ready now. Come on, you'll have fun, you always do."

"No, I don't!"

They climbed into the De Soto and drove

off. It was a long ride to the outskirts of the city and Wilfredo's anxiety receded as he looked out the window at all the cars and stores and people and buses belching out smoke. But, as the Ugalde mansion came in sight, it began to slowly surface. Even so, he was well mannered enough to not say anything rude once they disembarked and were greeted by the Ugaldes at the door. Also, the pretty grounds allayed his fears; they always did.

It was noisy inside, everybody talking at once, his parents, Sr. and Sra. Ugalde, Julio and his sister, even he joined in. Gradually, if the young boy had been capable of introspection, he would have realized that old patterns were reasserting themselves, with the women going off to one side, his father and Sr. Ugalde off to another to talk politics, while Julio and Wilfredo were told to go off to play. The younger boy did not catch a warning look that Ugalde directed at Julio, nor did anyone else. Nor did Wilfredo go off reluctantly with Julio in so far as children instinctively congregate with one another.

"Let's go play checkers," Julio said and sat down in another room, playing for half an hour. The older, taller, boy won one game right after the other, smirking all the while, then let the younger boy win one game only to win it back at the end. By then he was bored.

They went outside where there was a basketball hoop and shot a few baskets with Wilfredo giving a poor performance. Meantime, the adults stayed inside, yakking away.

"Say, I've got an idea," Julio said, grabbing a handball. "here, take this ball and try to hit me with it. I'll stand by this wall. We each throw five times. The one by the wall tries to get out of the way of the ball. We take turns. You go first."

Wilfredo had misgivings, but went along. He did not throw too hard, not wanting to hurt Julio and Julia easily evaded all five throws. Then, they switched places.

The smaller boy also evaded the first four, to Julio's surprise, but then Wilfredo now felt, rather than realized, that he was in a trap and so, was moving out of the way in fear. The fifth one connected and smarted; he yelped, but did not cry.

They switched places and Julio evaded the volley (the ball would bounce back). Then, they switched places again.

The ball now came hurtling so fast that they were a blur and connected each time with the young boy's body and face. Wilfredo first yowled, then cried openly, all the while trying to miss the ball, or at least catch it on the rebound. Worse, Julio did not stop, but went past the fifth throw and kept throwing it viciously at the smaller boy with a maniacal gleam in his eye.

Wilfredo's cries were finally heard inside the house and Sr. Ugalde stiffened.

"What's that? It sounds like Wilfredito crying," he said with a frown.

"Oh, it's nothing," his father said, "probably fell down and skinned his knee."

Ugaldo exited, leisurely followed by the others. Outside, looking at what was going on, he yelled out through clenched teeth.

"Julio! Stop it, you little---!" He advanced, instantly whipping out his leather belt, bury written all over his face. Julio froze, terror now showing on *his* face as Wilfredo kept sobbing.

"I told you what I'd do if you hurt that little kid again!" and he layed into Julio, catching his smartly across the face with the belt and proceeding to the rest of him, the others trying to calm him down, Wilfredo's parents most of all, saying that "It was nothing, really!" "You know how kids are," "Don't do it, chico, he didn't mean it" and the like.

Julio was exiled to his room to lick his welts, while the others resumed their conversation again, though feeling a bit awkward. Actually, the awkwardness was felt by the Ugaldes, while the Menendez were totally oblivious and carried on as if nothing untoward had happened. Wilfredo, who had now stopped sobbing, stayed close to them.

Finally, it came time to leave and the Menendez family drove away.

The long drive back was spent in talk between his parents while the boy, once again, looked out the window. All the passing scenes helped to alleviate his experience and began to subtly erase some of the sharper feelings. Almost arriving home, Wilfredo began to pay attention to what his parents were discussing. They were eagerly looking forward to next month. The Ugaldes had invited the whole family to spend the whole week with them at their ranch in Las Villas province.

THE LEMONADE STAND

It was the day of the much ballyhooed currency exchange. The Communists, having come to power less than two years prior, but not having officially proclaimed themselves yet as Marxists until they had consolidated their power, had followed the usual pattern that had occurred in other countries from China to Czechoslovakia to Russia. Among these changes was a currency change. The old Cuban bills, portraying the likenesses of José Martí, Antonio Maceo and Carlos Manuel de Céspedes, would be turned in, in exchange for bills having more revolutionary themes printed on them, at which time, the old currency would be deemed worthless.   A   few   diehards ("counterrevolutionaries") decided to keep the bulk of the old currency secreted away while exchanging just a few necessary bills, while still more courageous individuals not only kept the old currency, but even had American dollar bills and coins mixed with it, a sure guarantee to a trip to a prison if the secret police discovered the cache. In the spirit of total equality, every person could only exchange up to a certain amount of money, the exact amount having been determined by some illiterate Marxist while in a drunken stupor.

In the days to come, Juanito could not say exactly how the idea had first entered his head. Enough to say that when he leisurely walked over to where one of the numerous exchange centers were in Almendares to take a look---it was only two blocks away---and saw the long line of people patiently awaiting their turn in the hot tropical sun. It had reminded him of the time, not too long ago, when he and one of his friends had set up a lemonade stand in front of their houses in a nascent entrepreneurial spirit that all children get at some point in their lives. Unfortunately, there were no lemons to be had! Nor oranges! Nor Kool-Aid! Shortly after the revolution, all food had become painfully scarce, as the Marxist government rationed the scraps to the people while the Party members ate well, like pigs, "some animals being more equal than others" (Fidel, Raul and Che always seemed to have potbellies). So, the idea of a lemonade stand was simply not possible.

He suddenly had an idea and he ran all the way home, panting.

"Mom! Mom! Can I have your cigarettes?"

His mother looked at him. "What do you want the cigarettes for?" Even though she had quit smoking, she still had a few packs inside a chest of drawers. They were multicolored cigarettes that she had gotten years earlier and set aside, sold at a nightclub in town as curiosities because of the colors.

"I want to sell them. I want to make one of those little things that cabaret girls have and sell cigarettes to the people in line down there." He had seen many films.

"All right, sure, go ahead, you can have them," she said, amused.

Juanito went to the drawer and hurriedly opened it and took out the four packs and opened them. He thought that he could sell them easier if he sold them individually.

He then took a thick string and put a thumbtack at each end and attached it to one half of a broken briefcase. He then poured the cigarettes in it.

What else was in demand? Ah! Comic books! Comic books had completely disappeared and although he enjoyed rereading his supply of old comic books, the spirit of making money had completely come over him and he selected some of them for sale. He had no doubts that he would sell some of them since adult Cuban men loved to read comic books just as much as their children did. Juanito also knew that he could sell some cigarettes, since they were American cigarettes and he had heard adults asking each other if they still had any left and muttering when they did not.

What else was there? He was going to get the Gillette razor blades that his father still had, but there his father put his foot down. "No way! I can't get any more razor blades for blood or money! I said, no!" Juanito was not upset; he was having too much fun.

"How much should I ask for the cigarettes, Mom?"

"How about fifty cents each?" she suggested.

"Isn't that a bit high for just one cigarette?" his father asked.

"Oh, I'm sure that he'll sell a few. They're American cigarettes, you know. You can't find them anymore."

"I suppose," he shrugged. He had never smoked. Juanito went back to his hoard and rearranged it. On one side were the comic books, on the other the cigarettes.

Anything else?

Yes! He went back to his room and dug out a small book with the title of *Animal Farm.*

A couple of months ago, his father had picked out from among his library a few books in his possession, with titles like *The Great Swindle, The Bridge at Andau, Darkness at Noon, Fall of a Giant, The Little World of Don Camillo.* In the little patio in the back, away from prying eyes, he slowly tore up the pages and burnt each book.

"What're you doing, Dad?" the boy had asked him.

"Just in case," his father replied enigmatically.

"Just in case what?"

"Just in case the new Inquisition stops by."

Juanito did not understand what he referring to, but he did detect fear in his father. Just then, he had noticed *Animal Farm* with the animals on the cover and opening it and seeing a few cartoons of animals in it, and there not being any more comic books to be had, Juanito had snuck it away into his room while his father prodded the smoldering ashes. There, he had read the fable; some of it he enjoyed and some he did not understand it; he did not like the end because it really had no end and, besides, towards the end it was sort of sad. He then kept the book hidden since he was now afraid to return it and tell his father that he had taken the book, perceiving at the same time that the book was somehow dangerous and should be kept out of sight.

However, at this point, Juanito had completely forgotten the feeling of fear in his desire to make money and subconsciously came to the conclusion that the book was probably in demand. How to get it past his father? Ah! Put it under the comic books; and he did so.

"I'm ready," he announced.

"Good luck," his father said from behind the

newspaper that he was reading.

"Have fun," his mother said.

Juanito was out of his house, balancing his tray carefully and started walking towards the place of exchange. He really wanted to run there in his excitement, but then his merchandise would come flying everywhere. He walked fast and became more impatient as he rounded the corner until he was almost in agony. Presently, he saw the line of people and felt a little better, although he was still impatient to get there.

When he finally got there, he composed himself and arranged his tray. Most people were talking to each other about this, that and the other. A few adults in the line eyed him curiously. He was planning to go up and down along the line, announcing his wares, back and forth, back and forth. He decided to start right at the point of exchange and work his way to the end of the line. He began.

"American cigarettes for sale! Comic books! American cigarettes for sale! Comic books!"

There was a stunned silence in the crowd as they all looked with mouths open and eyes as big as saucers at the child slowly walked down the line announcing his wares.

Then he was mobbed.

He was suddenly surrounded by a forest of arms.

"Look! They're really American cigarettes!"

"Hey! It's a *Superman* comic book! And here's *Batman!*"

"And here's *Tom and Jerry!*"

"Hey, kid, how much you want for the cigarettes?"

"Kid, I'll buy the whole lot! How much you

want?"

"No, you won't! I want some too!"

"I'm taking *The Lone Ranger* to my kid."

"Sure it's for your kid."

"C'mon, kid, speak up, don't stand there like a statue with your mouth open, a fly will get in. Speak up!"

"Hey, it's *Donald Duck!*"

"Jesus! Look at this book! It's *Animal Farm!* I didn't think that there was one left in the whole island."

"What about it?"

"What about it? *What about it?* Don't let *them* see it, that's 'what about it.'"

"Here's *Uncle Scrooge.* I haven't seen one in months!"

Poor Juanito's brain had short circuited from the sensory overload. He had expected an occasional customer, like in his previous lemonade stand, not this! He could not see them all and was afraid that they would steal his things and he would be left without anything, crying; he also, at the same time, realized that he was also going to rake in the money; at the same time, he was also afraid that he was going to run out of things to sell.

He was totally confused.

"Come on, kid! How much you want for the cigarettes?" They were all off his tray and in his hands in front of him, waiting impatiently.

"Ah, fifty cents."

"Great, here!"

"No, I meant seventy-five cents! Seventy-five cents!"

"Jesus! You said fifty cents!"

"I meant seventy-five cents."

"Look, fella, if you don't want to pay him,

hand them over! I will!"

"No, I want them," said another one. "I only got two."

"No, I'll give it to him," he handed two bills over.

"Oh, no! I don't have change!" Juanito realized with dismay.

Other adults made change for him, while the ones with the comic books and *Animal Farm* asked how much he wanted for each one. Each time, he voiced a different price and they each handed over the money. A few even told him to keep the change, happy with what they had been able to obtain.

In less than ten minutes, it was all over!

He was cleaned out!

He had sold all of his merchandise and his customers were back in line, chuckling at the unexpected availability of these items, smoking the cigarettes with undisguised pleasure, or reading the comic books.

Animal Farm disappeared, nowhere to be seen, along with the man who had bought it.

Juanito felt good and excited and happy at all the money that he had made, but at the same time was disappointed that it was all over so quickly. He also had a feeling that he could have made more money if he had raised the prices, but that it now was too late and he wished that he had more cigarettes and books and comic books for sale.

Just then, he looked up and saw one of the uniformed Communists behind the table where the currency exchange was taking place looking at him with undisguised hatred and he became afraid.

He hurried home.

PEPITO AND MARTICA

"That's the really frightening part. The Owsla---
well, you can't imagine it unless you've been
there."
Richard Adams, *Watership Down*

Pepito was awake very early that morning
because of the smell. He had fallen asleep early last
night after a long day of constant playing, so he had
gotten sufficient sleep. His parents were awake and
at the table where he joined them for breakfast.
Breakfast was one slice of bread, toasted, with
butter. It smelled heavenly. His mother was telling
his father what a struck of luck it had been to get a
stick of butter.

"And I was just walking down the store
when the man put out a sign saying, 'We have
butter for sale.' You should have seen it! It was like
a swarm of bees! Everyone who saw him, ran, I'm
telling you, *ran*, to the store door and began to line
up. One man said that he didn't even know what
there was, that he'd find out when he got to the end.
I was lucky: I was fourth in line."

"Too bad that Ana wasn't with you," his
father said. "Why didn't you call her up to let her
know?"

"As soon as I got my butter, I called her
from the telephone in the store, but by the time that

24

she got there the line reached clear around the block and they had run out."

Pepito took a bite of the toast. The melted butter ran between his teeth.

"Hmm," he said appreciatively and his father chuckled at the sound. He ate the toast, relishing each bite.

"Would you like the rest of mine?" his father asked him. Half a toast was left over.

"Oh, yeah!"

"All right, let me cut off the edge where I ate so you won't get any of my germs," and with the table knife, he cut off a strip of toast that showed bite marks. He gave the rest to his son who gobbled it up. He himself ate the bitten strip.

"Mom, can I have another one? Please?"

His mother thought for a second and her husband nodded at her. "It's just that I'm afraid that he might get sick if he eats too many," she told his father.

"Well, just one more and that's it, all right?" his father said and before too long, another slice of buttered toast was in front of him, with the butter melting. Before too long it, too, disappeared. Pepito was full. It was a rare feeling.

It was a good feeling to be full. For a change.

"Now, go brush your teeth and scat! Go play," his father said.

Pepito did as he was told. He went out, taking his wooden top along. He looked around the street. There were no kids out playing at this time. Across the street and to the left, he thought that he saw a faced looking out the window at his house and withdraw inside. Even now, he thought, the window drapes looked out of line. The house belonged to the Hernandez family. On the garage door was pasted a brand new Revolutionary poster showing a cartoonish drawing of a man with a fierce expression and some words written alongside of it, with lots of primary colors.

Pepito walked the other way. He would now and then spin his top, first this way, then that. He tried several times to do the *cortaleza,* a sweeping spin that made the top skip down the sidewalk quite a long ways on its tip, like skipping a flat stone across water, before finally resting in one spot, spinning. He had not entirely mastered it, but this morning he did it eight times in a row and each time was good. He next tried what he had not been able to do even once and that was to pick up the top with the flat of his hand while it spun on the sidewalk. He tried it and the top toppled over. He spun the top and tried it again. And again. And again. And again. He could not do it. No matter how many times he tried it, he simply could not do it. But, many of the other kids could. A couple of them could even, after picking it up, throw the spinning top off of one palm and catch it in the other palm, still spinning on its metal tip.

"Hello, Pepito," a girl's voice quietly said behind him. He turned around and saw that it was Martica.

"Hi, Martica!" He was glad to see her. She was the same age as him (nine) and she was pretty. Pepito at one time had fallen in love with her, every time that he saw her pretty face. He had even told his parents once that he was going to marry her.

"What are you doing?" she asked.

"Oh, I'm trying to pick up the top while it spins on the ground, but I can't get it. It falls over. But I can do a *cortaleza* really good! Want to see me do it?" he asked, eager to show off.

"Sure," she said and he would the string along the grooves of the top. He demonstrated four or five times. Thankfully, he was able to do it each time, not once fouling up. They walked over to where the top was spinning.

"I'm getting really good at it," he said with a smile.

"What are you doing up so early?" she asked. "It's eight."

"I don't know, I just woke up," he shrugged, still smiling.

"Say, Pepito, what do your parents think of Fidel?" she asked. She tried to make it sound like she was asking what did they think about the weather, but somehow could not make it sound innocuous.

Pepito was immediately on his guard. His feelings for her vanished and he remembered that she was the daughter of Hernandez.

"Oh, they think that he's fine."

"Well, but what do they say about him?" she persisted.

"Oh, I don't know, I don't remember. I don't pay any attention." He gave the stock answer that his parents had told him to say if anyone---at school or out of school---began to ask him questions about politics.

"But do they like Fidel or not?" she kept on.

"Oh, yeah, they like him." He was nervous, a bit afraid.

He remembered whispers of parents being taken away at night, never to be seen again, merely on the strength of what their kids had let slip out. Some of the kids, it was said, had even deliberately denounced their parents to the school because they had been making anti-Communist remarks at home about the new regime.

Suddenly, he was angry. He didn't like Martica anymore. He looked up at her and he did not see her pretty face. Her prettiness was gone, somehow vanished, and those feelings that he had had for her had just now completely, permanently, evaporated. All he saw now was a very, very bad person. An enemy. A girl, but still an enemy.

"Why do you keep on asking me those questions?" he snapped at her, with anger in his voice He tightly gripped the top with his fist and advanced towards her.

"I was just curious," she said. It was now her turn to be afraid.

He said nothing further, nor did he spin his top. He looked around. They were standing beneath a small Revolutionary poster that had been posted on a garage which had a man's face fiercely looking down at them. The words in the poster extolled all good Communists to be on their guard against counterrevolutionaries and to turn them in to the secret police. Had he been old enough to know the meaning of the word "psychotic" he would have thought that it was very apt.

Almost all of the houses had a poster posted somewhere in their homes, compliment of Hernandez, who had put them up at night. To have been passed over was a signal that the particular home was suspect.

Their home had been passed over.

As he did not say or do anything, the silence and the inactivity became awkward. She was too young yet. She had much to learn. With practice, she would become better at it.

"Well, I better be getting back home," she

said. "Until later."

"Until later."

Pepito saw her retreating back towards her house and he knew, without anyone telling him, that she was going to report to her parents. Her parents belonged to the Neighborhood Committee, a local volunteer branch of the secret police. He felt something, but he was still young to stop and try to identify the complex feelings that he felt. Children often have that handicap. But, in watching her go, he felt something. He definitely felt something.

He, in turn, would have to tell his parents of what had taken place, so that they could be on their guard.

He looked up at the poster at the man's fierce expression. He looked around, particularly at the Hernandez house. Pepito, in a sweeping motion, raked the top's metal tip across that face full of hatred three times, defacing it.

Then, he resumed spinning his top.

A MISTAKE IN CLASS

I could a tale unfold, whose lightest word
Would harrow up your soul
Macbeth
William Shakespeare

The young boy stared at the cartoon, perplexed. His name was Eduardo and he had an issue of *Bohemia* in his hand. Only, it was not the same *Bohemia* that it once used to be. Not really. Although it had the same look and the same name, it was now . . . different. The words were different, somehow. The stories were certainly different. Even the usual cartoons in the last page of Cuba's national magazine were different.

For one thing, they weren't funny.

Or were they?

Maybe he just didn't get it.

Like this one, for example, it showed the Líder Máximo, the Maximum Leader, in a boxing ring with Uncle Sam, who was covered with bruises and had black eyes. The caption was the slogan that was nowadays going around, "Fidel, seguro! A los Yankees dale duro!" which translated something to the effect that Fidel should hit the Yankees hard.

In the past year, comic books had suddenly disappeared---you couldn't find *The Lone Ranger,* *Donald Duck and His Nephews, Batman,* or *Superman* anywhere. The television programs with animated cartoons had likewise vanished, replaced by government shows, which Eduardo's father called "imbecilic" and "grotesque" and Eduardo himself disliked.

Movies were no good, either. They were all Russian and had no story whatsoever; they were really stupid and a theater was lucky if there were three people seated in the vast audience hall; usually they were empty; even a Soviet version of Don Quixote, the Spanish language's most beloved work, turned out to be pure garbage. Even the mice ran out of the theater.

Even so, out of habit, and in sheer desperation, Eduardo checked the television each day at four in the afternoon for the cartoon shows that used to come on at that time and would never return again. He had searched all the stores for the nonexistent comic books, read the *Bohemia* cartoons and even in desperation, occasionally went to an empty movie theater---only to exit half an hour later in disappointment and boredom.

The boy concluded that the cartoon he was reading was funny. It had to be funny. After all, it was a cartoon. He just didn't get it.

He would have asked his parents to explain the joke, except that his parents didn't want him to read that magazine any more. They said that it was part of something called "brainwashing." Brainwashing was supposed to change you in some way.

And now, another idea popped into his head, one that had lately been recurring with more frequency: maybe his parents were wrong. Maybe they were mistaken. Just like he didn't get the humor in the cartoon.

They certainly didn't like the revolution.. Or its Maximum Leader. Behind shut doors and windows, they talked with some of their trusted friends and said bad things about the situation in the country. They also told Eduardo not to breathe a word of what he might overhear, for God's sake!

Eduardo kept quiet.

Except that, now and then, he had his doubts.

Maybe it was they who were in the wrong.

Maybe it was better if it was out in the open and it could all be straightened out.

*   *   *   *

*   *

Eduardo was in school now.

"All right, close your eyes now. Are they closed? No peeking now." None of the students in the classrooms were peeking. "All right! Now ask for God to bring you a toy right now." A few seconds passed.

"Open your eyes!" The children did so, and, of course there were no toys on their desks.

"All right! Close your eyes again! Don't look! I don't want to catch anyone peeking. Now ask for the Communist Party to bring you a toy. No peeking I said, Reynaldo! I mean it! I'm going to go around to make sure that nobody's peeking." A minute passed. "Open your eyes now!" And behold, in front of each child was a little, cheap toy. The children were delighted.

After they had played with the toys for about ten minutes, or so, the teacher spoke up again.

"Now, then, let's try this again. Close your eyes and wish for Santa Claus, or the Three Magi, whichever one you want, to bring you a toy. Close your eyes!" Half a minute passed. "Open your eyes!" The pupils saw no toys in front of them.

"Now, close your eyes again. Keep them closed and no peeking, or you'll get punished! I'm coming around to check. All right, let me see, all right, I don't see anyone peeking. Now, kids, again silently ask Fidel and Che to bring you a toy!" Another minute passed.

"Open!"

Another toy!

The teacher let the kids play with their tiny toys for a few minutes, then told them to put them away, so the class could resume.

His teacher then began talking about all the wonderful things that The Revolution was accomplishing. Now, vaccinations were in ice cream instead of painful injections, wasn't that nice? And a comrade nurse brought in those ice creams at just that moment for every student to eat. They didn't taste good at all, but it had been over a year since anyone had had ice cream (or milk; or sugar---in Cuba!), so it brought back memories.

The teacher---who was an amazingly fat woman in spite of the shortage of foodstuffs---was going on and on with her praises of the Communist regime.

Later, Eduardo would not be able to say why, exactly, it came about that he just blurted out, "My parents don't like Fidel. They don't like The Revolution, either."

Everyone had looked at him. The teacher, in particular, had looked at him strangely.

"Well, can you tell us more why not?"

"They just don't."

"Do you remember what they've said?"

Eduardo barely restrained himself. "No, not really." Then, "I'm not getting them into trouble, am I?"

"Oh, no! You see, Eduardo, perhaps what your parents need is to go to a Re-Education Camp."

"What's that?"

"Like school. But for grownups. Where they can realize the error of their ways. Then, they'll be able to appreciate the benefits that Fidel and The Party have brought about through The Revolution."

"Oh. I see."

The teacher suddenly dropped the matter and they were assigned some complicated math problems. She left the classroom a while later for a few minutes and returned afterwards. After the math problems, they went straight into history---the new, revised history, that is.

Half an hour before the bell rang for the end of the day's classes and they could all go home, the teacher asked Eduardo to come with her. He accompanied her into the hall, walking towards the principal's office and little Eduardo became worried that he was going to be punished for what he had said earlier in class.

"Oh, no, *chico!* Get that out of your head!" she reassured him. "You were very good in mentioning that in class and letting us know."

"Then, why are we going there? To see the principal?"

"Well, there's some people there that want to talk to you," she said, smiling, while opening the principal's office.

Inside the room, along with the principal, there were two men in uniforms. Eduardo had never before seen the uniform of the dreaded secret police, nor had his parents, but the expressions on their faces said it all and he suddenly, and without warning, burst out crying, thinking of his father and his mother and his sister and realizing, with a sinking feeling, that he had made a horrible, ghastly mistake.

TUNA

What you have to understand is that when we first came to America, we had just a little knowledge of English. I had learned mine from an ancient Berlitz book whose one feature, I remember to this day, was a tiny cartoonish drawing of a man on each page with an oversized balding head and spectacles that prevented his eyes from being seen.

The other thing that you have to understand is that after years of Communist starvation in Cuba, the stores had been empty of goods for all those years---all except those stores that were reserved for, as Djilas would say, the New Class, members of the Party. So that when we walked into a grocery store outside of Communist Cuba our eyes fairly popped out.

Anyway, within a few weeks after arriving, we had begun to develop habits and preferences for this, that and the other. For instance, tuna. We enjoyed eating tuna with rice and our favorite was the Bumblebee brand that we, for some unknown reason, referred to as "the little wasp," which, unfortunately, though the best was also the most expensive. But we also, from time to time, ate "the mermaid" (that was the Chicken of the Sea brand, which pictured a mermaid on the label) and "the beatnik tuna" (the Star Kist brand, which pictured Charlie the Tuna on the label). I do not want to give an idea that we ate nothing but tuna. We ate everything else, chicken, steaks, roasts, soups, salmon, etc.

One day, we found a new brand of tuna at

bargain basement prices. It was "the cat" brand tuna and they must have been having a special introductory price sale because each can was selling for an amazing twenty-five cents, in order to hook the customers, so that they would try it and switch brands. Well, we loaded up on our shopping cart! This sale was not going to last for very long!

At the checkout counter, the cashier, seeing the dozens of cans, made a comment about our haul. We told her that, at that price, we could not pass it up and we were going to stock up. But my daughter was frowning at her. She was the best in English.

"Excuse me. What did you say?" she asked the checkout girl.

"That you must have some very hungry cats at home."

"Why?"

The checkout girl, hearing our chatter in Spanish and my daughter's accented English, divined what had happened and spoke slowly.

"Because this tuna is for cats, not people. It's cat food. It's for cats, for your pets. That's why it's so cheap."

My daughter did not have to translate. For once, we had understood every word and we all burst out laughing.

We put back all those cans of cat food back on the shelf.

WELCOME

Omar had been in the United States almost two weeks. The English that he knew consisted of about a dozen words and phrases, which really means that he could not speak the language at all.

Omar was staying with his uncle in Ybor City until his parents could leave Cuba. His uncle had been living in America for many years and had offered his home to Omar and his family. The boy was glad to be where he was and so were his parents. Aside from his uncle, though, the boy knew no one else and, at times, felt lonely and homesick.

At this time, Omar and his uncle were sitting in front of his uncle's home, talking, as was the custom in Cuba, and one hard to follow in the new country since most American houses do not have a front porch where seats could be arranged for this purpose. His uncle's house did have one. They were talking about a little gift box that the boy had received from some unknown donors. These gift boxes, given to the Cuban refugees, though modest, elevated the spirit of the recipients, young or old. In Omar's case, he had gotten a gift box earmarked for a child and in it, much to his delight, was a comb, a handkerchief, four short coloring pencils, a little notepad, a toothbrush, a small tube of toothpaste, some candy, some chewing gum and a couple of small toys. These items, though, again, modest ones, had made his spirit soar. Unfortunately, he had no one to play with the toys, or to color with.

Omar wistfully looked up at a group of boys in the street who were noisily playing in brief bursts of activity, while talking with his uncle.

At one point, the boys had one of their brief lulls of activity, except that this time they looked over at where the uncle and nephew sat. They seemed to be talking about them. One of boys approached the porch and asked the nephew something in English. His uncle translated, smiling.

"He wants to know if you would like to play with them."

The boy jumped off the chair with a cheer and they both ran back to the group of boys, Omar almost tripping on the way.

One of the boys talked to him and the Cuban boy nodded, not understanding a *single* word spoken, although he said "OK" a couple of times whenever they asked him anything. Even so, he had a rough idea of how they were playing: there were two sides and everybody tried to get the ball.

Omar looked at the ball. It was strangely shaped, not round at all, but in spite of its shape, he realized that it was supposed to be a ball.

They took a long white rag and tucked it inside his pant's waist. He had no idea what it was for. No matter. He was enjoying himself already.

Two lines were formed and they pointed to a spot for him to stand, so he went there. He crouched like they crouched.

The lines bust into activity, then ceased.

This occurred three or four times.

On the fourth scrimmage, Omar actually reached the kid running the ball and he grabbed the ball and tried to wrest it away from him. At this, all activity ceased. Some of the boys looked surprised, then two of them laughed and then everybody laughed, not at him, but good-humoredly.

The boy who had approached him at the

porch now went to him shaking his head and talking, and seeing that he was not being understood, went through a pantomime whereby he grabbed the ball holder's white rag, threw it on the floor and then the ball was handed to him.

With a sudden "Ahh!" Omar understood, and the boys understood that he understood, and they resumed the game.

Since it was assumed that he would have been successful, anyway, his team got the ball.

Omar looked at who had the ball, then crouched again into his position. At the burst of activity, he whirled around, saw who had the ball, flew to his teammate, grabbed the rag and threw it on the ground.

Now *everybody* laughed hysterically. A couple of the boys were even rolling in the ground laughing with tears coming out of their eyes.

Nobody had to tell him that he had goofed.

Omar slapped his forehead. In a sudden flash of inspiration, he saw his mistake. He had to stop *the other side* from capturing the ball and he let them know in broken English that now he understood.

"I understand! I understand! Yes! Yes! Ok, Ok. I understand. Yes!" he said over and over to let them know. Once the boys recovered, the game resumed.

It went on for close to two hours. Omar fit in perfectly with the way that the game was supposed to be played; once the game began in earnest, it was as if he had been part of the group for months.

At sunset, they broke up and began drifting home. Several waved at him, saying, "Bye, Omar" and he was waving back and saying goodbye as well.

He straggled back to his uncle's house, tired, where his uncle had been keeping an eye on him. The boy was sweaty, scratched, tired and achy and he could not wait for tomorrow to come so that he could play again with his new friends.

A DAY EN UN RANCHO

I think that we had been in the United States for almost three years when my father was invited to a "ranch," what in Cuba we would call a *finca.* He was a doctor in a hospital where the patients were all soldiers. I mean soldiers that had fought in wars. It was called Veterans' Hospital. It was one of his patients there that had invited him to his "ranch;" we were invited too, of course.

Dad told us that he was a real cowboy, just like in the movies that we had seen in Cuba, which had Spanish subtitles. I knew that he was telling the truth because we were living in Oklahoma, and they were all around, so it was nothing new. Every day we saw them walking around in boots and blue pants and cowboy hats. Women, too, they were called "cowgirls." Nowadays you don't see them as often.

In Cuba, my father had also been invited to many *fincas* by some of his patients. I had ridden horses there past the palm trees and seen the sheds where the tobacco leaves were cured. At nights, there were times when we could see bats whizzing by and tarantulas walking over the porch and *cocuyos,* a kind of firefly (if a bat flew inside a *finca,* there was a general scramble to catch it, spread its wings so it would be helpless, light a cigarette, put the unlit end in its mouth which would clamp down on it and release it, watching the glowing point of light fly off into the night). They'd also have a feast of *lechon asado,* a whole roast pig, cooked over an open pit.

Oklahoma was nothing like Cuba. It was dry. It was hot. The soil was read, I mean *red.* And riverbeds were empty, dry and hard, like scars. Outside of the city, there were no trees to speak of. But, there were people who were farmers there. I don't know what they raised, except maybe rocks.

Anyway, my parents and my brother and I packed into the car and we set off that Saturday to see this *rancho*. Every weekend we would go ride around in the car, anyway, except that this time we had a destination. It was located somewhere between Norman and Lawton.

Oh, yeah, I forgot. Something else that was different. Cuba had hurricanes. Oklahoma had tornadoes. All the time it had tornadoes.

Anyway, back to the trip. Dad followed directions. Me and Manuel (that's my brother) guarded the map and the directions that the man had given him and we would watch out for landmarks.

After going through several dirt roads, raising a cloud of *red* dust behind us, we finally got there. One of the first things we saw was an oil well and the first thing that we smelled was crude oil. Crude oil smells like . . . crude oil. Can't compare it to anything else. It was strong, too.

The oil well wasn't like the oil wells that we had seen before in films. It didn't have a big tower with oil gushing out. Instead, it looked like Manuel's geologist hammer, only bigger, and constantly in motion, slowly going up and down, up and down, up and down, up and down, up and down. After a while, though, you got used to the sound that it made and did not even hear it.

Anyway, we got there and the patient and his wife greeted us. They had no kids. Manuel and I, we knew right away that we were going to be bored.

After a while, they put us on a couple of horses though, which were tame, they told my parents, and his wife rode with us. She never stopped talking but I don't remember one word of what she said.

We didn't see much while we rode, just a lot of leafless bushes and more red dirt. Manuel had hoped to see a rattlesnake. Near Lawton, there was a sort of state "park" (a park with no trees!) in a mountain in the middle of flat ground for miles around and in the park there were buffaloes and cows with *huge* horns that would at times rush at the car. Anyway, there was an Indian there that had rattlesnakes in cages and sold some liquid medicine.

We got back. It was time to eat and it was going to be a "bar-b-q." We had heard of "bar-b-q" before and seen the grills for sale, but this was the first time that we'd eat some and even see how it was done.

Anyway, the man put some round pieces of coal in the oven and squirted a lot of liquid from a small can into it, then lit the coals with difficulty. At first, there were flames, but then they dried out. And here was the strange part: although the coal wasn't on fire, it gave off heat. He proved it to us by having us hold our hands over the oven. Then he put a grill oven it and then put steaks on the grill. We were shocked to see that the man was going to do the cooking, but none of us said anything out of politeness, although his wife had cooked other things like potato salad, which tasted awful. Years later, we would finally accept the fact that in the United States, it is the man who cooks at the bar-b-q, just like also he is the one to carve the turkey, or ham, in Thanksgiving and Christmas.

We ate. The steaks were good, the potato salad awful. They had a picnic table outside and that's where we ate.

Manuel and I got bored again.

After that, the man let us shoot off his shotgun at some cans. That rifle had some kick to it!

It got dark and they went inside to talk. Me and my brother went in and out, in and out, looking for something to do. When it got dark, we could hear the coyotes howl, and that was really neat. And spooky.

At one point, I strolled over to the bar-b-q by myself, bored out of my skull, and looked at it. All of the round pieces of black coal were now gray, with tiny red bits in it, so I thought that they were burned out, although there was still some heat coming out of them. I picked up the can of liquid and gave it a big squeeze while looking close up at the gray ashes.

Big mistake.

With a *whoosh!* flames leaped up and so did I. I think I jumped six feet away from that "bar-b-q," scared speechless. I didn't even yell. For a couple of seconds I thought that my hair had caught on fire and I hit myself on the head with my hands in order to put out the imagined fire. Then the flames in the oven died down by themselves.

I was going to tell them what had happened then thought better of it. I might get in trouble for what I did. And, if I told Manuel, he would probably blab, I know him.

But, boy, was that scary!

I could have gotten burnt up!

For the next hour, even if I had tried I couldn't go back to being bored.

At that time, our parents *finally* decided that

it was time to go.

We didn't have any trouble retracing our way back home. Manuel fell asleep on the way back. Me, I kept thinking back at the explosion (*whoosh!*) and imagining myself covered in flames and hairless and without eyebrows.

Anyway, that was my first visit to a *rancho* in Oklahoma.

(Since then, I've heard of the phrase, "Be careful of what you wish for, you just might get it." Whoo, boy.)

FIGHTING FRIENDS

"Mister Abelson?" the secretary stuck her head at the doorway of the Vice Principal's office. "I was able to reach the parents of Juan. They said that they'll be here shortly."

"Both of them?" he asked, a little surprised.

"Yes, sir. I got through to Mrs. Vallejo, but she doesn't speak English, but she did know, or at least she's memorized, enough words to tell me to call her husband at work. She had the phone number memorized. I got through to Doctor Vallejo-"

"Oh? He's a doctor?"

"Yes, sir, a dentist and he said that he'd be here shortly, with his wife."

"Good Lord, Margaret, didn't you tell him that it wasn't an emergency?"

"Yes, I did, but he said that he'd come over anyway, that he wasn't busy."

"All right, thank you." He sighed as she withdrew from the door. He did not want to inconvenience the parents on something that was relatively minor. Still, at the same time, he wished that more parents were as involved with their children as were Juan's parents. The children would probably benefit as much as the staff, directly or indirectly. But, nowadays, they just saw school as little better than a baby-sitting service.

The two boys, both eleven years of age, were waiting outside, all scratched up and bruised, still smarting from the fighting that they had been involved in. The Vice Principal was surprised that it was these two boys who had been involved. Among their other good qualities, they were both well-known as being very easy going, very smart and the best of friends.

He went to the door and called in one of the boys.

"John? Come in." He noticed that both boys were far apart from each other. The boy went in and the Vice Principal closed the door.

"Johnny" he said as he sat down, "care to tell me what happened?"

"Mister Abelson, we were just out at the rec yard, talking and he hauled off and punched me for some reason! I don't know why! I tried to ask him while sitting out there and he won't say anything to me." The boy was evidently perplexed.

"Well, something you said, perhaps. Did you insult him?"

"No, we were just making jokes."

"Aha. And what kind of jokes?"

"All kinds. Mostly knock-knock jokes. I wasn't making fun of him. Honest!"

"I thought you two were friends."

"We were! I don't know why he hit me!"

"Mmm, go outside and sit down. And tell Juan to come in here."

The other boy came in, uncharacteristically surly.

"Well, Juan? What happened in the rec yard?"

"Nothing," he said, looking down.

"What do you mean, 'nothing'? Didn't you get into a fight?" The boy did not respond.

"Answer me!"

"Yeah, I guess."

"Well, what started it?" The boy shrugged his shoulders, still looking at the floor.

"I thought you two were friends."

Still that maddening silence.

So, the Vice Principal tried another tack.

"I contacted your parents and they're on their way."

That did it. The boy looked up at him, all trace of surliness gone, replaced by a look of worry. Abelson could not help but smile, even though slightly. "Go wait outside," he said, almost adding "and stew."

In a little while, Juan's parents came in. The father looked angry, the mother concerned and Juan, well, Juan looked worried, only more so now that they were there.

"Doctor Vallejo? I'm Phillip Abelson, the Vice Principal," he greeted them, shaking their hands, "Mrs. Vallejo." They now both smiled at him. "Won't you come in into my office?"

"Thank you for coming," he said as they all sat down. "We're a little puzzled as to why-"

"-Excuse me, what?" Doctor Vallejo interrupted with a heavy accent in his voice.

"We're puzzled, ah, a little confused---mystified."

"Ah, yes, *puzzled*," he said as if filing away that word for future reference.

"Yes, we're a little puzzled as to why Juan and John would get into a fight."

"Johnny *y Juanito pelearon?*" asked Mrs. Vallejo surprised. *"Un* 'fight'? *Pero son muy amigos."*

"Yes, they did get into a fight, in the recreation yard. One minute they were talking and in another they were fighting. It looks like Juan started the fight by hitting Johnny first. And it was a nasty fight, from what I heard. I wasn't there, so I don't know what triggered it."

"Excuse me, Mister Albelson, while I translate for my wife."

"Of course," he said and the Vallejos exchanged words. When they appeared finished, he went on. "Johnny doesn't know why it started and Juan will not say a word to me---which is very unlike him, he usually doesn't stop talking," he joked.

"Juan talks too much?" Doctor Vallejo said, scowling. "He interrupts teacher? Does not listen to her?"

Abelson saw his mistake. "No, no, that's not what I mean to say. I mean, that he's always talking with his friends or with a teacher."

"He talks too much."

"*Appropriately* so," he emphasized. "In a *good* way. We all enjoy listening to him, he's got a neat accent. Everybody likes to hear him speak. Believe me, he's fine on that point," he said reassuringly. "The other day, for example, I was told John told Juan that he was a real card. Juan was puzzled at that and he opened up his dictionary and read out loud the definition of a card: 'a stiff piece of paper.' The whole class got a kick out of that one," he chuckled. He looked up and realized that they were not laughing and it occurred to him that he was making things worse. "A 'card' is also a person who is humorous, has a sense of humor---is appreciated," he explained. Doctor Vallejo seemed to understand now and smiled.

"*Que dice?*" the mother asked, while the father once again translated at length.

"Excuse me, Mister Albelson, but my wife says something that is true. These two boys are good friends. Very good friends. Johnny comes over almost every day or Juanito will pay him a visitation at his home. He come to eat in our house, our boy goes to eat at his house. They play all the time together. He comes to play in our house, our boy goes to play at his house. They are very good friends. Ever since we moved here four months ago."

"Where were you before, then?"

"What?"

"Where did you live before you came here?"

"Ah, in Miami. For eleven months, almost a year. Before then, you know, we were in Cuba."

"Castro took over, what, three years ago?"

"Yes. Horrible."

"We don't get too many Cubans here in Emporia," he smiled. He was aware that the Midwest had been settled primarily by Swedes, Germans, Czechs and, of course, the Indians."

"Well, what you say about the boys is true here in school as well. They're always together. They're the best of friends. In fact, they are two of our best students: excellent grades, they behave well, they're sociable, they have good manners, everybody likes them both." The father, visibly proud, spontaneously translated for the mother, who nodded as she listened, "which is why this is, like I said before, a bit puzzling. And since Juan won't say anything, I thought that perhaps you could get something out of him."

"Excuse me, what?"

"Get something out of him---find out why there was a fight."

"Ah, yes!" the father nodded vigorously, scowling. He would get something out of him all right, if he had to skin the boy to get it out.

"This school is very strict insofar as fighting

between students, very strict and since Juan did start the fight, I will have to punish him. Yet, at the same time, I'm very curious as to the whole thing. Has he been having problems at home?"

"No-o-o, no problems," the father responded, thinking.

"Well. Let's get him in here and see if you can find out anything," the Vice Principal said, getting up. He opened the door. "Juan, would you come in here?" The boy did so. It was apparent that the wait had frayed his nerves. "Your father wants to ask you something."

"Why did you fight?" Doctor Vallejo asked in English. The boy looked around, hesitating, so the father almost growled at him in Spanish. "Quiero que me digas la verdad, que estoy muy bravo! ¿Por qué Uds. se pelearon?"

The boy hesitated for a second, then he blurted out, "Porque el me toco la cara!" and he scowled.

Both parents said "Ahhh," and pulled their heads up. They looked at each other, nodding.

"What? What?" asked Abelson.

"He says that the other boy touched his face," he said with a tone that indicated that this was a different matter altogether, now it made sense and was even justified.

The Vice Principal, frowning, went to the door and opened it. "John, come in here!" The other boy did so and the Vice Principal regained his seat. He looked at the two boys standing side by side for a second, then asked the one, "Johnny, why did you hit Juan?"

The boy's eyes opened wide. "But I didn't hit him!" he protested.

"He says that you did."

"I did not!"

The father asked his son, "El te dio en la cara, o te toco la cara?"

"Me toco la cara," he responded.

"Mister Abelson, Johnny did not hit Juanito in the face. He touched Juanito in the face."

Both the Vice Principal and the boy looked lost.

Then, the adult had an inspiration as a thought popped into his head. Something that he remembered having read once, long ago, somewhere, that in Thailand it was considered very insulting to touch a Thai on the head, also in Indonesia, and someone had told him that some Japanese men preferred their wives to give them a haircut rather than let some stranger touch their heads. But that was in Asia, not South America.

"Doctor Vallejo, in your culture, in your country, that is, is it considered bad manners if someone touches your face?"

"Oh, yes! Only a girl lets herself be touched on the cheek! If a boy touches another boy in the cheek, that means he's a girl, a, what is that word? I saw it the other day, ah, yes, he's a 'sissy,' a sissy, it means that he's a sissy, a girl. So, of course, Juan, he had to fight him." Both parents felt that their son was vindicated.

Vice Principal Abelson began to comprehend, but the other boy saw nothing but absurdity.

"But I didn't hit him!" Johnny finally blurted out.

"But you did touch him in the face, in the cheek?"

"Yes, I did. So what? I didn't hit him! I was telling him a joke and he didn't get it and I had to explain it to him and when he *finally* caught it, I said, 'Very good, Juan,' and patted him." He motioned the gesture in the air. "But I *didn't* hit him!"

The educator glanced at the parents and realized that they, too, did not understand. Neither did Juan. Nor did Johnny.

"Doctor Vallejo, Mrs. Vallejo, Juan, do you understand that in this country if a boy touches another boy in the face it doesn't mean anything?" They looked at him as if he was speaking another language. "You do realize that different countries have different customs?" The dentist and his son nodded. "And what is considered bad manners in one country may not be bad manners in another."

"Bad manners is bad manners. All over the world," the father said.

"Yes, that's true. But up to a point. But in certain other things, it doesn't mean the same here," he motioned with his hand a spot in the air, then moved it to another spot, "as it does here. Different languages, different weather, different laws, different customs." He looked at them. He still could not get through to them. It was as if they were deaf. Johnny too.

"It's the same with language. For example, the United States and England both speak English, but we have some words in this country that we use every day without problem, but which in England are very bad words. Even though we both speak English."

"Yes! This is also true in Spanish, you know," the father said. "I understand. In Spain and Mejico they use the name for a, a, ah, yes---a sweet---that in my country is a very bad word, very bad. And in Cuba and in Spain the word for insect is a very bad word in Puerto Rico."

"Exactly! You see?"

"Ahhhh," Doctor Vallejo let out slowly. It all finally clicked. He turned to his wife and started explaining. The Vice Principal turned to Juan.

"Do you understand, Juan? John was not insulting you. Here, in this country, it doesn't mean anything if one boy touches another in the cheek."

"Yes . . . I think so. I think I understand. But I still don't like it."

Was it his imagination, the Vice Principal thought, or does Juan now look thoroughly embarrassed?

"It's just a custom in your country that means something bad. Do *you* understand, John?"

"Yeah . . . I guess so. It sounds kinda funny, though. I didn't know."

"Well, men, you still have classes. Are you ready to shake hands and be friends again?" Both boys nodded. "OK. Shake!" The boys turned around and shook hands.

"Well, now, usually whenever there's a fight, I have to paddle the participants," and saying this, he withdrew what seemed to the students a gigantic wooden paddle.

Their eyes got really big. They had heard of this paddle and of his wielding it. "But seeing as to how it was all a misunderstanding, that won't be necessary" and he began to replace it in the desk when he stopped in mid motion, "unless you two are going to start fighting again."

"Oh, no!"

"No! No!"

"OK, then, you're dismissed. Go to your classroom. Oh, and Johnny? Don't do that again."

The boys left, much relieved. He looked at

the Vallejos. They were as amused as him. "Thank you both for coming, you helped to clear up the air."

"How you say? 'Clear up the air'?"

"Yes, you solved the 'mystery.'"

"Well, I'm glad that we could talk with you," Doctor Vallejo said, shaking hands. "Anytime, call us. For anything."

The wife touched him by the arm. *"Oye, chico, preguntale lo que paso antenoche con el bostezo. A lo mejor es la misma cosa."*

"Yes, that's a good question. Is yawning bad manners in this country?"

"Yawning? How do you mean? No, usually not. Why?"

"Two nights ago, we were on a visitation to a friend's home. I was tired and sleepy and I yawned many times and the man looked angry at me."

"Wait a minute. Was he talking to you?"

"Yes."

"Was he telling you a story?"

"Yes."

"Then, yes, he felt that you were being rude to him and that you were insulting him. If he was talking to you and you yawned, it meant---to him---that you were not interested in what he had to say."

"But that's not true. I was. I was just tired."

"It doesn't matter."

"Ah," said the husband. *"Si. Dice que si, que significaba ser maleducado."*

"Ya me lo supuse!" she responded, nodding vigorously.

"But only when someone is talking. Otherwise, it's OK."

"Dice que nada vez es cuando le estan

hablando a uno. De otra manera esta bien, no significa nada," he translated.

"Thank you very much. I'm glad that we talked with you," Doctor Vallejo said.

"Thank you," she said also and she waved goodbye as they left.

The Vice Principal returned to his office, sat down and smiled. He stared at the wall for a full minute and then he sighed.

MY WEIRD AUNT

Everyone has a weird aunt somewhere. That just simply seems to be a fact of life. It is as if when you come into this world God assigns you A Weird Aunt. Now, how weird she is going to be depends completely upon the luck of the draw. And, the way I see it, everyone is *entitled* to have a crazy aunt.

Aunt Josefina is my weird aunt. I loved going over to her house to visit her, which I could do anytime that I wanted to since she lived only a block away (that was before we moved away to another city). Sometimes, right after playing with my neighborhood friends, if I found myself near her house, I would stop on my way home and she would always give me a snack. She was always glad to see me. Once in a while, she would call up my mom and convince her for me to have supper with her, which I would, and then right afterwards we would catch a TV show, usually a comedy, before I had to walk on back home.

My favorite times to visit Aunt Josefina were weekend nights. She would get permission from my parents for me to stay overnight. Now, the reason that I particularly loved coming over on weekend nights was that there was always a late night TV show which we would stay up late to watch and which always had neat monster movies, or science-fiction movies in black and white way back from the Fifties and Forties, which would always give me plenty of material for nightmares later on that night. The show itself was hosted by some weird, creepy character who camped it up. He may have been Dr. Demento. I don't know. Anyway, I thought he was cool (later on, Elvira would become my favorite). I wanted to be like him and would at times talk in that sneering voice of his. Dad would remark at these times that it wasn't too late to replace me with another kid.

Aunt Josefina and I would watch these movies together and she would get as scared as I did. Anyway, during these marathon scary movie sessions, she would prepare a bowlful of buttered popcorn, or maybe vanilla ice cream, or even a whole package of Oreo cookies with cold milk. Unfortunately, there were times when the ice cream ended up in the ceiling whenever a monster jumped out to scare the viewer as I jerked halfway over the sofa. And on more than one occasion my aunt ended up covered with buttered popcorn.

During those times, I was in kid heaven.

Sometimes, I could even bring a friend over.

Now, what made Aunt Josefina deserve the title of my Weird Aunt?

My, my, where to start?

Well, for starters, she had aligned her bed in a strict north-south axis. This was in accordance to the Earth's magnetic flux, she said, and, according to her, this alignment of her bed was conducive to her being at one with Nature. The trouble with this was that her bedroom was rectangular and not very big, while her bed was enormous and, more importantly, the shorter end of the rectangle was the north-south side. Additionally, she had planted her bed in the middle, right where the bedroom door was, so the first view of her room was the back side of the headboard blocking the entrance to the bedroom.

When my father one day pointed out to her that, according to geologists, the *magnetic* north pole was not the same as the *geographical* north pole, and, that the magnetic pole had in millennia past wandered from one location to another, he threw my aunt into a tizzy. For my part, I had this vision of a human magnetic pole hitchhiking a ride from an Eskimo's dog sled over the ice floe.

And then there were the dragons. *Somewhere* she had picked up a book that told her that dragons---as in flying, fire breathing dragons---not only had existed in the past, but were still around, but in some sort of "astral plane," invisible to mortals, that they were ordinarily well disposed towards people and occasionally helped out in human affairs in subtle ways, I suppose like guardian angels (though disliking human technology), and that a person could communicate with dragons on an emotional level, if well disposed towards them and open minded. My aunt was totally uncritical of such a concept and embraced it wholeheartedly, without any reservations. That's when she started collecting little statues and candles shaped like dragons.

She also dangled a hollow wooden pyramid over her bed, about a foot wide.

In addition to the alignment, Aunt Josefina had faith in the power of crystals and every night, just before going to sleep, she would place small pieces of quartz, amethyst, topaz and other, I don't know what, crystalline minerals over her forehead, her closed eyelids and her belly button. Then, lying in bed at night in the dark, she would make a circle with her thumb and her middle finger, and slowly and respectfully repeat the following mantra over and over again:

"Tuga-wuga-gaba-bada."

"Tuga-wuga-gaba-bada."

Some nights, for variety, she would change it to:

"Dima-duma-bon-bon."

"Dima-duma-bon-bon."

In the dark, I could hear her from the sofa in the living room doing her "Tuga-wuga-gaba-bada" or "Dima-duma-bon-bon" routine until she would drift off to sleep, at which time her mantra got blurry and her "Tuga-wuga-gaba-bada" became "Fuzza-wuzza-huba-huba" and her "Dima-duma-bon-bon" lost its edge and turned into "Bizza-buzza-ding-dong." In the morning, she would pick up the scattered crystals off the bed and floor and remark how refreshed she felt, thanks to those crystals. She credited her good health all these years to the power of crystals and the magnetic alignment of her bed. As proof, she cited the undisputed fact that she had never had a serious illness or gone to the hospital in eleven years.

"Josefina," my dad told her once, "I have a more efficient, proven method of staying in perfect health. Every three months, I periodically change the oil in my car with one leg off the ground while wearing my polka dot shorts. I've never been seriously ill for fourteen years, nor gone to the hospital. So! Explain *that* away!"

Aunt Josefina got angry. "You never take anything I say seriously! Why can't you keep an open mind?"

"Wait a minute, I just *told* you that my method of keeping healthy is better than yours. With your way, you've been free from serious illnesses for eleven years; my method has kept me healthy for fourteen years. Why can't *you* be open minded? If you were open minded, next Saturday you'd be out in my driveway changing the oil in my car with one leg off the ground while wearing a polka dot pair of shorts."

I think that out of all her peculiarities, the one I enjoyed most was that of the UFOs. She had been a follower for many years, closely following "developments in the field."

I used to read many of the books that she had collected and they *were* fun to read. These books detailed cases where glowing extraterrestrial vehicles manned by aliens (this was always assumed) had been sighted by different people. Sometimes they had landed and the aliens had been sighted on the ground.

What my Aunt Josefina was particularly interested in were the cases of abductions. They had to do with people who had been traveling in a deserted road and a ball of light followed them, got bigger, paralyzed them and landed. Then, little aliens with black almond-shaped eyes would march out of the UFO and the people would, like sleepwalkers, follow the aliens back into the craft and were either medically examined, or taken for a ride before being released. Sometimes the abducted people remembered, sometimes not and had to be hypnotized later by hypnotists in order to remember details of the hours lost during the encounter.

As I said, she was especially interested by the abduction cases and she would often discuss them and would end by wishing that she would be one of the lucky ones to be taken up on a UFO. She used to be filled with wonder at what the experience would be like. She was certain that the aliens were peaceful and curious.

"Oh, I'd give anything to be taken up on a

UFO by aliens!" she exclaimed at my home one time after going on at length about the subject before the whole family.

"I'd give anything also," my Dad said.

"You'd like to be abducted by aliens?" she asked him surprised at this change in him.

"Oh, no! I meant that I'd give anything to see *you* abducted into outer space by aliens," he clarified. "I'd pay good money to see that. It can't happen too soon as far as I'm concerned!"

It so happened that, one day, there was a convention in town on UFOs that weekend. Aunt Josefina said that she was going and would take me along. She was very excited about it. I looked forward to it, too.

The convention was in a hotel. There was a huge room with tables near the walls where people were selling things. There was also, in the center, more tables arranged in a circle containing more stuff on sale, with the vendors behind the tables. We strolled around. Most of them sold books and magazines. A couple sold only books that they themselves had written about their experiences with flying saucers, which they would be willing to autograph if we bought copies. Another one sold casts of aliens' heads that she had put together from descriptions of eyewitnesses; they all had a domed head and big, black eyes. One man had tapes for sale, lectures spoken by an alien in its language; he let me hear part of it; I couldn't understand any of it and I thought that it sounded a bit like him.

There was also a lecture room. A couple of persons from the dealer's room were scheduled to speak. When we went in someone was already giving a lecture on some guy named George Adamski who, it seems had been a hot dog vendor at Mount Palomar and been taken on a ride on a flying saucer by angels.

The lecturer that Aunt Josefina had particularly come to see was Madame Jakomsky. My aunt was really very eager to hear her. I don't remember much about her lecture other than she had been abducted five years ago and that for the last year they had come back to visit her once a month. They would signal her by flashing a strong beam of light through her window. Madam Jakomsky would get up and walk out of her home like a somnambulist and once outside, she'd be levitated into the awaiting UFO. Then, for the next hour or so, they would talk about all sorts of things over tea and cucumber sandwiches (Madame Jakomsky had a noticeable English accent).

Aunt Josefina came away from the convention happy and enthusiastic. She had come away with the impression that alien abductions were common, everyday occurrences and that her time to be taken into a UFO was imminent. To her delight, as luck would have it, that night's late night movie was *Close Encounters of the Third Kind,* one of her favorite films.

Now, at this point I have to point out that our local police department had recently acquired a helicopter and the police were happy with their new toy, taking it up at the slightest excuse. Or without an excuse.

And . . . as luck would have it, the two occupants wore white helmets which had large dark plastic circles to slip over the eyes (keep this in mind).

Later on that night, just as she had drifted off to sleep, towards the last "Bizza-buzza-ding-dong," there came into our neighborhood the police helicopter, apparently on the search for some burglar, or some fugitive, or something of the sort. It was hovering from one house to another with its powerful searchlight trained on it. Well, that powerful beam of light shone right through my aunt's window and the backwash of the helicopter blades made the branches forcefully rustle against the window and the wall.

Aunt Josefina jolted straight up from a sound sleep with a gasp, *instantly* convinced that her big moment had arrived, that aliens in a UFO were looking for her, indeed had chosen her, specifically, for an abduction.

Unfortunately, in the intake of air that had gone with the gasp, she had inhaled one of the quartz crystals that had become dislodged when she had suddenly jerked up her head, and was stuck in her throat sideways.

She was now coughing violently, panic stricken, and stood up on her bed in a flash with the further calamity that her head was now firmly lodged inside one of her hanging pyramids that she used to dangle over her bed, obstructing her vision.

Throughout all this time, however, was her foremost preoccupation that the aliens would not wait long for her and depart, with the result that she might miss out on her own abduction.

Still coughing and gagging, she stumbled out of bed and out of her bedroom, trying to make her way to the back door. The crystal she had already swallowed, although she still coughed and gagged, since it had scratched her throat on its way down. With her arms out, what to her mind must have been somnambulist fashion (Madame Jakomsky was still in mind), thereby keeping to the script as much as possible, she stumbled out of the house with the hollow pyramid still firmly lodged on her head. She could now feel the backwash from the helicopter and hear noise which was, of course, the noise that a UFO makes when hovering, as well as see the bright light all around her (the spotlight was now trained on her by the occupants of the helicopter who must have been flabbergasted at the apparition coming out of the house). Since she could not see directly above her because of her makeshift hat, she bent down and looked up. She could definitely see something above her, but details eluded her. For one thing, she caught a glimpse of one of the occupants who, because of his headgear (remember?) now definitely looked to her like one of her aliens. She straightened back up and raised her arms beseechingly. I guess she was telepathically communicating with the aliens to come take her away.

The crew of the helicopter, on the other hand, had no idea of what to make of this apparition below them and kept their searchlight aimed at this . . . thing.

I think that *they* thought Aunt Josefina herself to be an alien from outer space!

They hovered, wondering whether to call for backup help with shotguns in dealing with this alien (there was nothing in the regulations on how to deal with pointed-head aliens from outer space). However, since it had not made any threatening moves, the pilot decided that the wisest thing to do was simply to quickly quit this neighborhood, which they began to do right away.

Aunt Josefina kept her arms up in the air, had abandoned telepathy, and was now shouting, "I'm ready! Take me! Take me with you!"

I rushed to her aid and had her bend over so

I could yank off the pyramid from her head, which I did and in so doing we both fell on the ground in a sitting position. She searched the sky for her vanished UFO.

It was gone.

Lights were coming on in our neighborhood.

I really did not have the heart to tell her what had really happened, so I told her that yes, it had been a UFO, but I had not gotten a good look at it. Her momentary disappointment dissolved as she accepted the fact that, after all, she had indeed been through a great adventure. Aunt Josefina now began to tell me about the telepathic messages that she had received from the aliens during the event, with their telling her to go outside the house, that they meant us no harm, that they just wanted to communicate with her and that they would be back some day.

For many days thereafter she was positively ecstatic, thinking of herself as one of the chosen few. And anytime that she heard the helicopter way off in the distance, she thought that they were coming back for her and she would get ready and began packing a suitcase with clothes, just in case the aliens wanted to take her on a long trip this time.

Anyway, like I said, I didn't have the heart to tell her what had really happened and I never have.

And I also did not tell my dad.

HUMMINGBIRDS

In the apartment complex that we lived in, aside from the usual amenities, there was an accidental perk to living there. There was a pair of hummingbirds that used to frequent the grounds. Whether they frequented the area because of the abundant flowering greenery that was part of the apartment grounds, or whether they had nested somewhere in the complex, or whether the apartments were in a direct line with their travels, the fact of the matter was that they were often seen, almost on a daily basis.

It goes without saying that the residents of the complex were happy at being able to boast to their friends at work and elsewhere that there were hummingbirds where they lived. And it also goes without saying that they got much pleasure at seeing the two hummingbirds flitting about. Sometimes they would fly down the walkway in a blur that reminded one of silent, yet harmless, bullets. And sometimes they would hover over one spot, changing positions every now and then. Tiny and fragile, they were pretty and they were cute. Mothers would point out the hummingbirds to their children if they were flitting about, and husbands, after a grueling day at work, would enter their apartment smiling, saying that they had just seen the pair as they walked up from their car.

Like most apartment complexes, there was a swimming pool located in the center. There was also a Laundromat. One day, as the maintenance man was inside the Laundromat, it so happened that---for whatever reason---one of the hummingbirds flew into the room.

The maintenance man, upon seeing the hummingbird, immediately shut the door and tried to catch it, chasing it all over the room and using his sweat stained shirt as a net.

There was an older boy there in the room who had been sent by his mother to check on the wash.

"Leave it alone! Leave it alone!" he yelled in a very distressed manner to the adult, as the latter chased the poor, terrified creature all over the room.

The hummingbird had never been trapped nor chased before in its entire life and it was frantic with fear. Inevitably, it was caught as it tried to go through one of the glass windows.

"I always wanted to hold a hummingbird in my hands," the man explained as he scooped up the struggling fairy.

"Why don't you let it go? See? She wants him back," the boy pleaded, pointing out its mate flitting nervously outside the window, looking in.

The maintenance man maneuvered his fingers gently and produced the hummingbird like a trophy, holding it by each wing. But, the terrified creature continued to frantically struggle for freedom and, in doing so, broke a wing. Both the boy and the adult were dismayed.

"You broke its wing!" the boy said, shocked, unbelieving. He repeated it again, this time in an accusatory tone. "You broke its wing!" and added with a hiss in his voice, "You idiot."

Feeling remorse for the accident, the maintenance man took the injured hummingbird to his apartment. He put it in a birdcage with plenty of birdseed and water, where it thrashed around in fear whenever anyone would come near and died a few hours later.

Its mate disappeared from sight and was thereafter never seen again. But, the man could, from now on, boast that, at one time, he had held a hummingbird

SONYA THE CAT

Sonya The Cat was three years old. That was her full name and title, not just Sonya, but Sonya The Cat. She was Abyssinian royalty. She thought so, anyway.

Sonya The Cat and I were friends. Yes, friends. That's the only kind of close relationship that one can have with a cat, you know.

Cats. They're independent, they are dignified, they are affectionate, but they also expect *respect.* And some are downright haughty. Like Sonya The Cat.

Oh, yes, and clean. Cats are definitely clean. When they go to the bathroom, they make it a point afterwards to clean themselves and the spot.

Not so with dogs. Dogs are not clean. When you step out in the yard, you had better be careful of where you are stepping or you will be sorry. Oh, you will be so sorry!

Nor are dogs independent. Or dignified. You can describe a dog many ways, but "dignified" is a word that simply does not come to mind when you think about a dog. There is nothing dignified about an animal that is forever grabbing every opportunity to stick his big, wet nose in your crotch.

Sonya The Cat would never do such a thing.

Nor would she indulge in that repulsive canine pastime when dogs jam their noses deep into the hind ends of their fellow dogs and inhale deeply until they get cross-eyed.

I ask you: would a cat do such a thing?

Of course not!

And fawning. Have you ever seen how a dog fawns? It would fill any self-respecting cat with disgust! And no matter how hard you beat a dog, it comes crawling back to you, tail wagging and tongue hanging out, slobbering in anticipation. What masochists! And it is this that precisely appeals to certain individuals. These human beings are so obnoxious, so abusive, such a sorry excuse for a human being that they have few, if any, friends. And it is precisely these persons that love dogs, because no matter how crass, how abusive, how neglectful, how pathetic they might be, a dog will always accept them and fawn on them and welcome their presence.

But cats? I can just picture myself raising my hand to strike Sonya The Cat. She would stop whatever she was doing and give me a withering look that would make me realize that I had already overstepped my bounds.

However, I must say that one day I played a trick on her Serene Highness, for which she almost never forgave me.

It was nothing, really.

She just blew it out of proportion.

Actually, it was simply that I had caught her in an unguarded moment. I had simply gone around the house and there she was. Except that instead of sitting regally on the porch calmly surveying her domain, she was stalking birds. Yes! Stalking birds! Just like any regular old alley cat.

I approached, fascinated.

The birds, a few yards away, ignored me just as they ignored Her Sublime Highness. As for her, she was too far gone to notice me at all, even if I had come in blowing a tuba.

What concentration! Her eyes were as big as

saucers. She crouched. Yes, that's right, she hugged the ground, actually oblivious to the dirt. Her eyes were fixed on a few birds in one corner of the yard and she would stare at them as if hypnotized, then, in a fluid motion, she would advance noiselessly for a few feet, paw-over-paw. She would then stop and stare at her intended prey and you could almost hear her making calculations under her breath. It was remarkable. Nothing else existed, but the birds. Her eyes never left the birds, who apparently were making it a point to ignore her. Then, she would advance again for a short spurt of paw-over-paw. Then stop. At a certain point, known only to her, she got ready to spring. Her back paws lifted up and alternated going up and down in anticipation for the burst of speed. She tensed up. Her tail twitched. Her haunches were up. Her ears pointed forward.

It was then that, having crept up, I reached out my hand and goosed her.

"Wooga-booga!" I yelled.

Sonya The Cat sprung straight up in the air by almost three feet, hind end first. And, to add insult to injury, she violated the Primary Feline Directive and landed flat on her stomach, each leg perpendicular from the body.

When she saw who had done this to her, she gave me the dirtiest look that a cat can give a human being.

I tell you, if looks could kill . . . .

But, that was only for a moment. She quickly gathered herself up and with as much dignity as she could muster, walked away pretending nothing had happened, nothing at all, making it a particular point to ignore the contemptible, braying jackass rolling around on the ground next to her, clutching his sides laughing and tears coming out of his eyes.

It took me a long time to make it up to her, but after many sardines and saucers of cream (not milk), she finally forgave me.

We never bring up the topic and we never speak of it.

Every now and then, though, I snicker whenever I remember the episode and I have to restrain myself from, once again, sneaking behind her and yelling, "Wooga-booga!"

GOING CAMPING

His son, Joel, had been with his father for a week when he began to pester him in earnest now.

"Dad, *when* are we going camping?"

He could not put it off any longer and resigned himself to the inevitable with a sigh.

"This weekend, OK?" (after all, he *had* promised).

"Yeah!"

Joel was undeniably happy about it. Dad was lukewarm at the idea. He had never gone camping before, had no interest in it, had never even been even mildly curious. Although an athlete in several sports (volleyball, tennis, scuba diving, fencing, karate), he was strictly an indoors type of person. A homebody. The idea of sleeping in the grass, in the heat, and with bugs and snakes around, when one had a perfectly fine bed in a perfectly fine house, seemed to him the height of absurdity.

But . . . he could not say "no" to his son, since David saw Joel so rarely now that his ex-wife had moved out of state and Joel came to visit only during the various school vacations.

Before coming down for the visit, Joel had phoned and asked for a camping trip while staying with his father. It seemed that he had joined the Boy Scouts months ago and they had gone camping. Joel had liked the experience.

"OK, big guy, you're the expert," David said to his son. "Let's go down to K-Mart and buy whatever it is that we need to get. You tell me what we need." And they drove to the store, David taking thirty dollars along for just that purpose.

As they went from item to item to item to

item to item to item, David began to get a shortness of breath; then he began hyperventilating. His eyes began to bug out. Two store clerks stood by to administer CPR the second that his body would hit the floor.

He had abandoned the idea of just thirty dollars for a credit card that would pay the additional costs, the card shaking in his hand as he paid for each item in the different checkout counters. A passerby thought that he had Parkinson's Disease because of the way that his hand trembled.

They bought a lantern. With kerosene.

They bought fishing poles. And reels. And a tackle box with tackle inside. And a cleaning knife.

They bought charcoal.

They bought insect repellent and mosquito netting.

They bought sleeping mattresses.

And extra pillows to take along.

They bought lighter fluid for the charcoal. And a portable grill.

They bought canteens and flashlights and batteries.

They bought a cooler.

They bought a first aid kit.

By the time that they got to the actual tents, David was on his last legs, wheezing. He stared at the prices of the tents.

He keeled over onto the floor.

Immediately, the two clerks were beside him. One of the two clerks, however, had the idea that CPR involved taking off the patient's shoe and then blowing air on the big toe.

The other clerk stopped and just stared at his toe-blowing colleague. Then, realizing that the prostrated man was on the verge of passing out and on to the next world without having bought the tent, he began to lean forward in order to administer CPR. However, David took this to mean that the male clerk was leaning over to kiss him, whereupon he rabbit-punched him and the clerk went down, knocked out cold. Then, realizing an odd sensation by his foot, he looked down to see the other idiot earnestly blowing air on his big toe. A quick jab with his heel at the clerk's jaw collapsed the offending toe-blower.

David got up. "Son! Look at the prices of these tents!"

"Dad! These are really good prices! We paid a whole lot more when I went camping before."

"Really?" he asked, unbelieving.

"Really."

Dad made a face, then picked up a boxed-up tent and put it in another shopping cart (by now they had two full ones).

After paying for this last item, the credit card could not take the strain anymore and disintegrated, crumbling into dust, right in the checkout girl's hands.

After dropping off the equipment at their home, they went to the supermarket and bought two sackful of groceries for the camping trip and two bags of ice. The ice was put in the freezer at home and the food in the refrigerator.

To Joel fell the task of coming up with possible camping locations. He first suggested Tok-sheek West Park, ten minutes away.

"Wait a minute," his father said, "Tok-sheek West Park is inside the city limits. What's the point of 'roughing it' inside a city park? And besides, that's the place where there was a chemical spill years ago that they tried to bury with a mound of sand and built a children's recreational sand lot over the spill."

"Yeah, I remember," he continued. "The authorities first got wind of it when all the owls lined up on the sidewalk humming the theme from *The Bridge Over the River Kwai.*" He frowned. "They couldn't hold a tune, though. But they did march right down to the pond and kept on walking along the bottom, humming that tune, hoping to get to the other edge of the pond. You could tell where they were by the little bubbles coming up to the surface. The bubbles ended right in the middle of the pond."

"Nope," he decided. "Rule out Tok-sheek West Park. What's next?"

"Well," Joel continued, "outside of the city parks, there's Ticks Lake National Forest as the closest, but that's ninety-eight miles away."

"Is that the closest?"

"Yep."

"That's it, then. Let's pack clothes and shoes in the bags. Maybe take a Frisbee and some gloves and a baseball. We leave tomorrow morning." He frowned and stared hard at his son. "On a Saturday. My day off. When I should be resting."

David was awakened in the morning by his son shaking him.

"Dad, wake up. We gotta get going. It's already six AM."

A groan escaped him and he put a pillow over his head. Joel shook him some more, this time vigorously, but stopped when he heard a snarl coming out of his Dad and one eye staring out malignantly at him from under the pillow.

"I'll get breakfast," Joel volunteered and

judiciously left his father to get up at his own pace.

They began loading up the small car. They put in all of the food, clothes, sports equipment and camping equipment. They added blankets, just in case it got cold at night. By the time that they were through, the rear fender scraped the pavement from the excess weight.

"I think we need a bigger car," his father said. "Or maybe a truck."

"Dad, we don't have to go it you don't want to," Joel suggested.

"Oh, sure! *Now* he tells me!" His father looked at him. "No! We're going camping! Whether I want to or not! And I'm gonna like it, no matter how much I hate it!"

David began rearranging things in the car so that the fender stopped scraping the pavement.

"Joel, I think that we'll be able to make it and have plenty of room if we just left you behind."

"Would I fit if I left the Frisbee behind?" his son asked.

David did some more rearranging and Joel did not have to be left behind. Nor his Frisbee.

The journey up to Ticks Lake National Forest was a very pleasant one.

"Are we there yet?"

"Soon, son, soon."

"Are we there yet?"

"Soon, son, soon."

"Are we there yet?"

"Soon, son, soon."

Once they finally arrived and slowly drove down the forested paths, they both became very excited.

They found the registration office, parked and went in to register.

"And do you have a reservation?" the park ranger asked.

"You need *reservations* to go camping?" David asked unbelieving. *"Reservations?* As in dinner reservations? As in theater reservations? You actually need reservations?"

"I'll take that as a 'no,'" said the ranger and looked over a map of the camping sites. "All the choice sites have been taken, but I can put you in #27. It's Primitive Camping."

David did not like the sound of that and asked him, "What *exactly* is primitive camping?"

"Oh, just roughing it," the ranger replied blithely and gave them directions to #27.

#27 was on the far side of the park. One had to park a long distance away from the site itself and cart all the car's contents at a ten minute hike.

Joel and his Dad each made five trips unloading the car and transporting the contents to the site. At the end, they sat on the equipment, panting and wheezing and drenched in sweat.

#27 was just a patch of bare dirt surrounded by forest. In the middle was a burned out spot, doubtlessly the spot of previous campfires.

After recuperating, they set about erecting the tent. After that particular wrestling match was over, an hour and a half later, they sat on the equipment, panting and drenched in sweat.

After recuperating again, father and son went for a stroll along the paths. That was very relaxing. They heard birds. They saw a pond and felt the cool breeze. For the first time Joel's father was happy at having come; he was enjoying himself immensely.

Presently, they returned to camp and since it was nearly noon, they set about building a campfire.

Now, all it lacked was a fire.

"Joel, hand me the matches."

"I don't have them."

"Well, get them."

"Where are they?"

"I don't know. Where did you put them?"

"I haven't seen them. Dad, didn't you bring any?"

"No, didn't you?"

"No. I thought you did."

"Oh."

They stared at the charcoal, hoping that it would light all by itself.

"OK, no problem. We'll just go borrow some matches from one of the other campers."

Not being particularly hungry, anyway, they leisurely strolled over to the camp area that they had passed earlier. It was a long walk. This particular area was not designated Primitive Camping. The vehicles could drive right up to the camping site, there was an electrical outlet available as well as a permanent grill. One of the campers readily gave them a box of matches for them to keep.

They strolled around the area, looking at the different campsites without actually staring. For the first time in his life, David noticed the RVs. Really noticed them. Unbelievably ugly and rectangular, their gas consumption must be nightmarish. Yet, they were a miniature mobile home, having bunk beds, a kitchen, a small refrigerator, a microwave, table, even a small television, all of it powered by the available electrical outlet at the camping site. David could not comprehend the logic of going camping in the wilderness yet carrying a microwave, bed, and television along with you.

As he was having these thoughts, a

Winnebago that had pulled up discharged a middle aged man, obviously happy at having arrived at his destination.

"Beautiful place, isn't it?" he asked David as they walked by, his hands affectionately patting his own stomach.

"Certainly is," he answered back as they walked past.

They were quite a ways from the man when a sound made them turn around. The man was collapsing onto his knees, making a gurgling sound as he did and with his eyes bugging out. He collapsed totally to the ground, wheezing with effort, each breath seeming to be his last.

David and Joel ran to where the high pitched wheezing came from and looked down helplessly at the man. He couldn't be choking because there was noise coming out of him and besides, he had not been eating anything, so what on earth was wrong with him? Maybe a heart attack?

At this point, the man's wife burst out of the RV running towards her husband with a First Aid Kit in her hand. She broke it open, took out a pack of cigarettes, lit one and stuck it in her husband's lips. The man sucked at it greedily. Slowly he calmed down.

"Too much fresh air," she explained to the mystified onlookers. "The shock of it was just too much for him. He gets careless and doesn't take it gradually." By now, the cigarette was spent and she lit another one for him. Slowly, the man got on his feet, well, though a bit wobbly.

Joel and his father went back to their campsite, the latter shaking his head in disbelief.

After lunch, they went fishing at the pond. On the way over, David noticed for the first time the flies occasionally landing on him and Joel. They were not the ordinary houseflies but were more colorful. He swatted them off, realizing with a shock that the flies were feeding off of them. Like most people, he had always viewed flies as unsanitary nuisances rather than predatory or parasitical. He whipped out the insect repellent and put some on Joel's arms and torso which now had small red bumps where the flies had bit him, as well as on himself. With the insect repellent on, twice the flies landed, thankful for the extra flavor. Dad and son took turns slapping each other on the back and arms, Dad getting a little bit too carried away with the slapping, by Joel's opinion.

They caught some fish but none was a keeper. And in spite of the fly swatting, it was enjoyable. They spent the whole afternoon that way, casting and swatting, casting and swatting. They also talked about a lot of things.

That night as they prepared for sleep, they found that there were some further unpleasantness awaiting them. Laying on the bedrolls, they could feel every tiny twig or pebble, no matter how small, and because their weight rested on the twig or pebble, its actual seize seemed much bigger, so they both spent the first hour or so trying to locate and remove the offending objects. Next, they discovered that a few mosquitoes were inside the tent with them and their humming kept them awake (it was like being inside a drum---the sound was magnified); worse, their not humming *really* kept them awake because it meant that the mosquitoes had landed and were about to bite them, no doubt attracted by the insect repellent. When they turned on the lantern, the mosquitoes could not be seen. Or heard. Dad finally hit on a solution. Rolling up a towel so that it became hard, as soon as he heard the humming he twirled it above them like a propeller. Within minutes, the tent was mosquito free.

They finally slept.

It was towards midnight that David awoke upon hearing noise nearby. With eyes closed, it sounded like Joel was trying to find something in the dark. He opened his eyes and saw Joel sleeping next to him. He groggily turned his head around and came face to face with a masked midget having a pointy nose. David made a lunge for the little thief, screaming for his son to wake up.

"Joel! Wake up! We're being robbed!"

It became a madhouse inside the tent. At one point he was able to land a punch on the dwarfish thief, who squealed in pain and tried to fight back.

"No, Dad, it's a raccoon!"

The tent collapsed on them, further confusing matters. The raccoon, having been punched on the snout, decided that it was not going to take that treatment from no oversized human, and leapt to the attack and bit David's earlobe. David screamed and leapt up, the raccoon hanging on to the ear. Then he tripped and the raccoon decided to make a run for it.

For the next hour and a half, David and Joel tried to erect the tent back up. Finally, they succeeded and they collapsed on their bedrolls. Ten minutes later, the raccoon came back, followed by its brothers. In a coordinated effort, they bit through ropes and pushed over a pole at the same time, collapsing the tent once more. The raccoon vandals retreated, giggling.

David whimpered.

The next morning, they woke up and fixed up the tent. They were getting really good at it by now with all the practice. It was then that they remembered having bought mosquito netting and having left it in the car. It would have kept the mosquitoes out. Maybe not.

They were about to fix breakfast when they realized that the gang of raccoons had carted away all of their food for one of their notorious raccoon parties. Even David had heard of the all night raccoon parties, where the drinking and carousing went on, each raccoon doing an imitation of a camper; sometimes on these occasions they ever wore clothes for greater effect and would dance to music from stolen radios.

In the car, all that was left was a jar of bitter olives for breakfast.

Father and son ate the olives.

Their lips puckered.

Then they picked off the red ticks hanging from their bodies. The ticks, like the flies and mosquitoes before them, had decided that the two humans were the equivalent of an all-you-can-eat restaurant. Joel put a match to each tick. He enjoyed hearing them scream.

"And they don't even have vocal cords," he mused.

"No, but they do have a mouth! And I got the bite marks to prove it!"

They decided on a hike and were rewarded in sighting deer, hawks and eagles. And flies. They swatted a lot of flies off each other.

The hike put them in a good mood, though, and they even fished some, in the hopes of catching their lunch, but this time the fish were not biting.

Father and son returned to their camp by noon. Since they were hungry but had no food, they both decided to break camp and eat something on the way home. The arduous process of carting everything back to the car began---minus the food.

Panting and sweating by the side of the car, the last piece of camping equipment was stowed away in the car.

"I guess that you don't want to ever go camping again, eh, Dad?" Joel asked his father.

David took a few seconds before answering. "You want to know the truth? I had fun. In spite of everything, I had fun."

"Really?"

"Really. In fact, I want to do it again. Not right away, mind you," he added quickly, seeing Joe's face and cutting him off before he suggested the next weekend.

"I mean, after all, we already have the equipment. It'd be a shame not to use it again. And next time, we'll know what problems to be on the lookout for. Yes . . . I definitely want to go camping again."

"All right!" Joel shouted.

"Well! Ready to head on out?"

"Yes, sir!"

David turned around just as Joel screamed out, "No, Dad! Look out!!"

David barely had time to see the skunk as it reared its hind legs and shook its tail at him.

He caught the full effect of the skunk's spray on his face.

CULTURE SHOCK

From Topeka, Kansas, to Miami, Florida, there is no straight superhighway, or, for that matter, any other type of road. If one wishes to travel on this type of highway, then one must go due south on U. S. Highway 35 into the stinking wasteland known as Texas until it crosses U. S. Highway 10, then make a ninety degree turn due east to get out of Texas as quickly as possible, before something bad happens, towards Florida. But, there is no such superhighway traveling the hypotenuse of this right triangle. And it was down this weaving hypotenuse of two-lane highways that the Nunez family was traveling on their way to a two-week vacation in Miami. Although speed is sacrificed by not taking the four lane superhighway, there are many other compensations, including bypassing Texas and avoiding contact with its boorish inhabitants, always a bonus for the unwary. Additionally, and some would say foremost, it being a better scenery, particularly when traveling through small, quaint towns. They were passing through one just now.

"Look at that," remarked the elder Nunez to his wife. "That's one of the great things about this country! No matter where you go, or how small the village, it always has its paved roads, its post office building, its little city hall and its traffic lights. And everything is clean. Not like it was in Cuba. Out in the country, in the small towns, it was a pigsty. Just like a century or two ago," and he shook his head in disgust at the memory.

The family making the pilgrimage to its roots in Miami was the husband and wife, Conrado and Xiomara and their twelve year old Manolito.

The youngster had come to the States when he was eight, early on when it was still possible to send children out of the country before the Communists got their hands on them. His parents had followed months later.

The trip was a long one and conversation rose up and down, with long gaps in between and jumping from one topic to another. After one such gap, with his mind wandering as he drove, Conrado remembered a visit of a week ago and snorted. "I still can't believe that insurance agent," he said.

"Mmm?" she said, interrupted from her own thoughts and then she remembered. "Ah, yeah."

This was what had happened. An insurance agent, an acquaintance of his, had called up Nunez at work to offer him life insurance and he had agreed to meet the agent at home after work. The salesman gave him his sales pitch, showing him the advantages of switching policies. Everything was going smoothly, the customer was very receptive and had agreed to switch insurance companies. The agent, pleased, went on to suggest that he could also include his wife and/or his son with their own life insurance policies, with Conrado as the beneficiary. And, as soon as he had said that, he realized that something was very wrong, for the elder Nunez was no longer smiling, but was, instead, tightlipped and frowning.

"What kind of a suggestion is that?"

The agent blinked in surprise.

"What kind of a man do you think I am?" Mrs. Nunez was also frowning, albeit not as deeply.

The agent stammered. "But, but, a lot of

people have their whole family insured."

"No, sir! I'm not going to be insulted! I'm not an immoral man! No, sir! Do you think that I want to benefit from my wife's death? Or the death of my son? You're being very insulting, sir! Yes, sir, that's what you're being!" His arm was waving around in emphasis.

Not knowing when to leave well enough alone, the agent tried to explain, sinking deeper into the quicksand and continuing to prod the death taboo. "It's not for benefiting anybody, Mister Nunez. The money would be for the purpose of covering funeral expenses in the event-"

"I said no, and I mean no! So, don't talk to me anymore about this!"

"Very well," he meekly agreed, barely rescuing his sale.

Xiomara just shook her head, remembering the visit. They exchanged a few comments on the incident and the car became silent once more, each one left to his or her own daydreams.

Manolito stared out the window and, as they passed farmhouses, he saw poultry and wondered if once in Miami whether there would be any cockfights that he could go to since there were so many Cuban refugees there. Even in the capital of Havana, in wealthy suburbs, many children raised roosters in their back yard as pets in order to compete with the other kids. Manolito had fond memories of his red rooster that he had left behind; it was the champion of the block.

It should be said, however, that the boy had become thoroughly Americanized and had few memories of Cuba, although the ones he did have were strong ones. Like the one just now, as they passed a stand selling fireworks for the Fourth of

July, which created a chain reaction of associations in his mind. They would be missing the Fourth of July parade back in Topeka, which would be no great loss. All "parades" in Kansas, indeed, the whole Midwest, from North Dakota to Texas were dismal, pathetic affairs. Regardless of the occasion, they were all unbelievably pathetic, consisting of a few noisy high school bands, interspersed with convertibles carrying schmucks waving at the crowd, with the parade ultimately petering out at the end. Sometimes they went to Wichita during the Fourth and it was just as dismal. No floats. No speeches. No raffles. No dances. No grand fireworks. It was pathetic. Parades were supposed to be emotionally cathartic, but these parades left everyone feeling empty and embarrassed.

On the other hand, carnivals in Cuba . . . now *there* was a parade! It was one of the few strong memories that Manolito had.

Of course, now with the joyless, fanatical Communists in power, full of hatred towards everything, the carnivals, like everything joyful in Cuba, had gone down the tubes.

For his part, Conrado was puzzling over a conversation that he had had with the mechanic at the gas station that he frequented a block away from their home in Topeka. He had taken his car to the shop for an oil change and a tune-up just prior to the trip. After many months of patronizing the station, Nunez had expected a "special price," that is, a reduced price, to be offered by the owner. None was forthcoming. Finally, this time, upon seeing the same amount as always for a tune up and oil change, he had asked outright for a "special price," not angrily, mind you, but definitely insisting. The owner looked at him blankly, not comprehending what on Earth he was alluding to. What was a "special price," anyway? What was that in reference to? He scratched his head in the American gesture of confusion and Nunez drove off, upset, after paying the bill, leaving the attendant wondering how in the world he had offended one of his regular customers.

As for Xiomara, she, too, was deep in thought, a little worried. Several years of living in Kansas had changed some of the habits among the Cubans living in the state, whether in Emporia, Wichita, Topeka, Newton, Manhattan or Kansas City. And she had to admit, deep down, that some of the changes had been for the best. For example, the old habit of dropping in on friends, unannounced, had been gradually abandoned; nobody really liked being surprised by people (even if they were good friends) who were under the assumption that the recipients of the visit would be ecstatic in seeing them again, irrespective of any plans that the victims themselves may have had.

Another habit that had slowly, and thankfully, gone by the wayside was that of insisting on paying for the whole tab whenever two or more friends got together in a restaurant. This had occurred, traditionally, even when two or more very large families had run up an enormous tab. The head of each family would insist that the other side was their guest and the grabbing back and forth of the check---with loud protestations and even the children making furtive grabs and bringing the check to their respective fathers---was always a lively episode. And a costly one. That custom had gratefully also faded away.

Nonetheless, Xiomara wondered if those customs still lived on in Miami.

The car slowly wove through the streets of Miami, as Conrado tried to follow the written directions that he had received from his cousin, Francisco. As they passed several streets, Manolito looked around. There was something odd about this place, he felt, but he couldn't put his finger on it.

They passed many stores with signs in Spanish rather than English. Several older women walked down the sidewalks carrying opened umbrellas as shields against the sun, even though it was not raining. This never happened in Kansas, *in Kansas,* not even in August.

A man noisily spat on the sidewalk and Manolito almost gagged.

The boy got the handwritten map from his father to help him out and read out the landmarks to look out for. He noticed that the address was 4772 and that the sevens were crossed.

They finally found the house and Francisco and Paula came out to meet them, noisily greeting them and hugging everyone, examining Manolito and loudly exclaiming how much he had grown. For his part, Manolito did not remember having ever met her.

Within minutes, they were inside sitting down drinking little cups of the strong Cuban coffee, loudly interrupting each other and talking about the other relatives who lived in New York. Paula and Xiomara mentioned several persons that they had known in the past. It seemed that both women came from the same town, Jagüey Grande.

Before too long, Manolito began to get antsy, hearing them talk endlessly about people he did not know and had no interest in whatsoever and he just had to get out of there, so he went outside the house "to look around." Once outside, he felt calmer, less nervous. He could still hear them talking inside, even though he was standing all the way outside one the sidewalk. He frowned. Americans were quieter, more subdued, especially Kansans. By comparison, Cubans seemed to be in a perpetual state of hysterics. While the Latins' visage was always animated, many Kansans were stone faced; you could tell them that a tornado had carried off their homes and their kids and not a trace of emotion would cross their face (not even if you told them instead that the twister had only carried off his fat wife, to which you would expect at least a smile of relief).

But to get back to Miami . . . .

Manolito got tired of loitering around and began strolling down the street. Unlike Topeka or Wichita, Miami had sidewalks in residential streets, so he did not have to walk in the path of cars. He was grateful for that.

There seemed to be a couple of stores at the corner and he strolled over, yet became uneasy as he got closer, because of the noise in one of the stores; apparently, there was a stereo and the speakers were blaring. The teenage boy shook his head. It was Sunday. In any, every, city in Kansas it was so quiet on Sunday that you could hear a pin drop two blocks away. On those days the cities looked like one of those sci-fi flicks where the population has vanished into thin air.

He entered the small store and looked around. It was so different. Almost all of the products were alien to him. One wall was stacked with boxes of weird produce (including thick tree roots!) inside cardboard boxes, another wall had a counter with cut meats behind glass, but the butcher section was out in the open instead of behind closed doors. The little grocery store was shabby---not dirty, mind you, but indisputably shabby. The boy was not used to that. American stores were immaculate. You could practically eat off the floor. He got out of there and went into the next store.

This store was really strange. Eerie. It had dried up weeds for sale, along with a multitude of different candles and saints' statues. There were also those bizarre pictures of Jesus that he had seen before for sale in frames: they were those repulsive renditions showing Jesus as a blonde woman with a sparse beard. Manolito had no idea what this was all about, but he did know that he didn't want to have anything to do with it and exited.

At one spot, in one of the stores, he noticed that there were four older men gathered around a table playing dominoes with animation in their moves.

He avoided the store with the blaring music and strolled back to the house and went in.

"I was so worried for you guys," said Paula to his mother, "that something may have happened on the way. Imagine! I had a dream last night, I dreamed of a cup of coffee with clouds of milk in it!" Xiomara gasped. "I told Francisco this morning, didn't I?" Her husband just snorted contemptuously and resumed his conversation with Conrado.

Just then, their teenage daughter, Elena, came in, back from visiting her friends and was introduced all around. Manolito stifled a laugh; she was pretty and barely on this side of obesity. She had smooth round cheeks, seemingly about to pop. What had made Manolito almost break out with laughter was that in the moment that he saw her he had an irrepressible urge of sticking an apple into her mouth, thereby completing the picture of a cute little roast pig.

For her part, upon hearing him talk to her (in English, of course), Elena giggled.

"You talk funny," she told him in English.

"What?"

"You talk funny."

"Funny? How?"

"Like a hick. You got a hick accent. A Cuban with a hick accent." She giggled some more.

Manolito did not laugh, but was, instead, surprised to hear that he had an accent when he himself could not hear it (next day, and apart from their friends, his father would praise Elena's beauty to Manolo, implying that they should date, to the young boy's horror that his father would even think of matching him up to such a lardball, not aware that to Cuban men, fat women are attractive).

With Elena home, it was decided to dine out and they all piled into one car, very crammed. As they drove off, they all proceeded to talk at the same time. Worse, they also switched on the radio and to Manolito's surprise, heard the disc jockey scream, yes, *scream,* nonstop (in days to come, he would come to know that this was not a bizarre, isolated case; Latin disc jockeys *screamed* at their audiences).

By the time that they finally got to the restaurant, Manolito was a nervous wreck.

But that was not the end of it.

Once in the restaurant, the waitresses (or even the customers) would yell out to each other across the booths. Even the older Nuñezes found this unnerving; like their son, they had gotten used to going to a nice, *quiet* restaurant in Kansas and speaking to each other in a soft voice instead of hearing everybody else's conversations and the waitresses' comments.

However, the food served helped to soothe everyone's nerves, not the least Manolito's, for the food was indeed outstanding. Cuban cuisine is one of the best kept secrets; few who sample it come away not hooked to it. The end of the meal saw a satisfied pair of families, whose two husbands now began to wrangle for the tab. Unlike previous endless friendly bickering, it was resolved surprisingly quickly by Nunez asserting, "All right. But next time, I get the tab." Manolito felt so full that he did not even mind the ride back with all the noise.

When they returned to the house and entered the porch, Paula screeched and yelled out, "A witch!" She pointed to the wall and Manolito's mother joined her. "Get it away! Get it away!" The boy looked at the spot where the women pointed, but all that he saw was a very, very large brown moth, really huge. Aside from its unusual size, it was just there, nothing else, and he realized, with an overwhelming feeling of embarrassment that it was indeed the large moth that the two women were hysterically referring to as . . . a . . . witch. Yes. A witch. A witch!

A witch!

The adult men laughingly brushed it off and the moth fluttered away, but not without passing by the women, who shrieked as it did so.

Manolito was glad that he was in Miami where none of his friends lived, otherwise he would have burrowed into the ground like a mole, out of sight, from sheer embarrassment.

Once inside, coffee was brewed and served. Then, with Paula's announcement that it was time for her *novela*, the women withdrew to an adjacent room where she switched on the radio to listen to an audio soap opera. She filled in the background for Xiomara's benefit, who for years in Kansas had been starved for a *telenovela*.

In the living room sat his father with Francisco. His father was telling his cousin about a friend of theirs in Wichita who worked for Cessna. He was ridiculing him because he was in the habit of saying to Nunez, by way of conversation, that "We're now going into overproduction" or "We're doing very good with overseas sales" and "We're looking into other types of designs." The use of the pronoun "we" was to them incomprehensible and they disdainfully interpreted it as an affectation. "As if he owned the company!"

It seemed to Manolito that his father and Francisco were missing an important lesson here, but he was too young to pinpoint what it was exactly and so, just got angry and he went outside.

By the third day, the boy was crawling up the walls and he was now constantly pestering his parents to go back home. He was on edge and restless and he told them that he was bored and homesick. What to his parents was a breath of fresh air to him had become a constant source of low level irritation, all the worse for him in not being able to realize, exactly, what the problem was.

In fact, one afternoon, the two women came back from a visit to a santeria and Manolo learned with horror that some witch doctor had waved a killed rooster by the neck around their heads several times while spitting in their faces . . . and that they had paid for that!

This is not to say that the whole time was spent in misery. Far from it! Being reacquainted with Cuban music (like Benny More, Celia Cruz and Gloria Estefan) was a delight. Listening to Three Skates daily on the radio had him doubled up with laughter, holding his sides, it hurt so much to laugh. He enjoyed playing *tute* and *brisca* with the playing cards from Spain, which were so different from *regular* cards. He also learned and thoroughly enjoyed playing dominos. Encountering a banyan tree one day sparked off nostalgic, long-buried memories. Likewise, going to the beach evoked an overwhelming, almost tearful reunion in the whole Nunez family, as if a long lost brother had been found.

And then, there was the food. Apart from regular lunch and dinner, Manolito let himself go, continually snacking on forgotten fruits like guava, mamey, papaya and the diminutive Johnson bananas, sweets like *capuchinos* and *buñuelos,* drinks like Hatuey *malta, batido* and *guarapo* and sandwiches like Midnights and Flying Saucers. At the rate that he was going, he would not be able to snicker at Elena much longer.

In between, however, he was intensely restless, nervous, like a migratory bird kept in a cage. It was as if a switch was turned on whenever his concentration was not on food, the beach, the music, *tute*, or Three Skates.

He pestered his parents so much that Conrado several times threatened to use the belt on him.

Even so, Conrado agreed to leave three days

ahead of time. Truth to tell, the parents were also becoming homesick. So they went on a shopping spree for supplies, the father buying bottles of anisette, records and books in Spanish, while the mother bought a huge amount of yuccas, plantains, coffee, Hatuey *maltas, capuchinos* and Midnights and *Bustelo* coffee. Knowing that they were leaving soon only made Manolito that much more restless, so that he only finally calmed down when he was in the car on the way back.

When they finally got back to Kansas, to the small city of Topeka, he felt an enormous relief.

Naturally, none of the *maltas, capuchinos,* or Midnight sandwiches made it that far, the last one disappearing somewhere along Mississippi.

And the really odd thing was . . . as soon as he returned to Topeka--- that very same day in fact---the boy missed Miami and wanted very much to go back.

THE CITIZENSHIP ORAL EXAM

There were close to a hundred well-dressed people in the lobby of the courthouse, applicants for American citizenship, along with their families and a few friends. Among them, there was a wide representation of races and nationalities: Nigerians, Filipinos, Lithuanians, Koreans, Palestinians, Ecuadorians, Jamaicans, Vietnamese, Chinese, Britons, Hungarians, Chinese, Czechs, all of them--- and their descendants---destined for "the melting pot." There was a mild excitement among them as they viewed each other with some amusement and curiosity as they mingled and met each other and learned where each one of them originated. A few secretly felt a bit guilty at switching allegiances although, to tell the truth, they had done so long ago without realizing it because America has the unique talent, or secret, of easily welcoming immigrants and making them feel at home, like they belong, and the thing is, it is done so quickly and without really trying. It just happens.

Off to one corner, waiting to be called in for their oral exam was a mother and her teenage daughter. They were not mingling as the others were. The daughter was giving her last minute pointers.

"Mom, remember: Woodrow Wilson took America into World War I in order to establish the League of Nations---that was the first UN---and to make the world safe for democracy."

"Well, it didn't work, did it? I mean, the last part."

"That's not important now! And FDR--- Roosevelt, who was a relative of the previous president, Teddy Roosevelt---took us into World War II when the Japanese attacked Pearl Harbor without a declaration of war."

"Was he the one that went to Cuba?"

"No, Mom! That was the previous one, Teddy Roosevelt, and he wasn't president at the time!"

A woman came out of her office and called them over. She led them to another room, bare except for a table, some chairs, an American flag on a pole and a photograph of the current president, hanging on the wall. The woman then left them, exiting through the other door, opposite the one they had come in.

"Ok, Mom, sit down!" the daughter told the older lady, who complied.

"Oh, Olga, I'm so nervous!" she wailed. It was true that she had been driving her daughter crazy while they waited.

"Don't be! Remember everything that we went over."

"I hope that I don't forget."

"Look, this is the last step for becoming an American citizen. We took care of all the rest, the paperwork and all. They're just going to ask us about American history and how the American government works, we pass and then we go on in a little bit to the swearing in ceremony."

"Good, that's good. I want to vote. I want to vote in the next election and get that fool out of the White House. But, *chica,* what if I forget? What if I can't remember?"

"Just don't get nervous, Mom!" Her irritation flared up again. If you get nervous, you forget! I read that somewhere. It's like an electrical power surge in a computer wiping out the memory. Besides . . . you know how you get when you get nervous! So-don't-get-nervous!!"

The mother looked down and to one side, meekly chastised. "Ok," she said, in a little girl's voice.

The doorknob rattled as it was being turned.

"Here he comes now," the teenager announced, excited, and both of them straightened up. A tall man in his late forties, dressed in a suit and carrying some papers, entered. He appeared to be in a good mood.

"Good . . . morning!" he exclaimed.

"Good morning!" they both answered back.

"My name's Abraham Apostolopoulos. And you are . . . ?" he left the question hanging as he looked over the papers.

"I'm Olga Pérez Jimenez and this is my mother, Maria Pérez Jimenez. We're both here for the citizenship exam."

He put the papers down. "All right. Both of your papers are in order. It will be an oral exam, but it has to be given to each of you individually, so if you'll step outside, I'll begin with your mother."

Olga began to leave, looked back at her mother. *"Buena suerte, mami,"* she said in a soft, encouraging tone, and left the room.

"Gracias, chica."

Mister Apostolopoulos smiled down at her, trying to make her feel at ease, then began to read the question from a sheet of paper. "All right. Who was the first president of the United States?"

"Jorge Washington. The tall man."

"How many states are there?"

"Fifty."

"What city's the capital of the country?"

"Washington D.C."

"Who is the president at this time?"

"The idiot."

Apostolopoulos shook his head as if he was brushing off an insect. "Beg pardon?"

"Eh? Oh. I mean, George W. Bush." All of a sudden, a thought crossed her mind. "You like Cuban food?"

"What? Oh, I don't know. I've never tried it. Is it like Mexican food?"

The woman instantly became angry, agitated.

"What Mexican food! No! Mexican food is peasant food! Chihuahua food! They eat with their hands, they don't know how to use a knife and fork, they never learned!" She straightened herself. "And it's all the same thing: beans, lettuce, tomato and ground meat in a tortilla! They fold the tortilla one way and they call it an enchilada. They fold it another way, it's a burrito. They fry the meat instead of grounding it up and they call it a fajita. The make the tortilla hard and they call it a taco. They open it up and they call it a taco salad. It's all the same! There's no variety! They got no imagination! And that guacamole! They make a paste of it and it looks just like baby poop!" She took a breath. "Do you know what *burrito* means in Spanish?"

The examiner, amused at her outburst, shook his head. "No. What?"

"Donkey! You eat donkey meat when you eat Mexican food! In a burrito!"

Mister Apostolopoulos was skeptical of her assertion, but decided not to start a debate. "Well. That was interesting. Shall we get back to the exam?"

"If you want to."

"What's The Bill of Rights?"

"That's what you have to pay each month for using electricity."

"What??" His head jerked up.

"Mine's too high for the last two months. I call them up, but it's like talking to a brick wall. Can you help me with my light bill and talk to them?"

"Not . . .light . . . bill," he patiently explained, "but The Bill of Rights."

"Oh, yes!" The lady realized her goof up and laughed at herself. "You're right." she looked to one side, amused at herself and chuckled again. "Light bill." She chuckled again.

"What's The Bill of Rights?" Mister Apostolopoulos repeated the question, as patient as ever.

She knew the answer now that she recognized the question and answered quickly. "Freedom of speech. Freedom of writing. Freedom to get together in groups. Freedom to arm bears . . . ."

"What? What? What was that you said? What was the last one you said?"

"Eh? Oh! Freedom to arm bears," she informed him. "Seems to me a little silly. Why would you want to arm bears? I think it makes more sense to give arms to people so the bears don't eat their legs." She made a face. "Besides, bears are too stupid. They don't know how to use guns." She looked up at him beaming. "It's a good thing for us, eh? I don't know. There's no bears around here, anyway. Except in zoos."

The examiner stared at her, expecting her to

own up to making a joke, but nothing was forthcoming. His staring made her nervous. Finally, he spoke.

"My . . . God. You're serious. You're really serious. It's such an old joke. And I thought that you were pulling my leg!"

"Eh?"

"It's not freedom to arm bears! It's freedom to arm bears---I mean, it's freedom to bear arms! Now you got me saying it!" Flustered he was.

"Ahhhh . . . . That makes more sense. The other way---that's silly." She frowned. "What means, exactly, 'bear arms'?"

"That you can own a weapon."

"Ahhh," she understood now, nodding her head. "You sure you've never had Cuban food?"

"Positive!" An edge was beginning to creep into his voice.

"Well, if you like that Chihuahua food, you'll love Cuban food. It doesn't have donkey meat."

He sighed.

"Ok, let's wrap this up, shall we? Who wrote the Declaration of Independence?"

"Thomas Jefferson, the tall redhead."

"Good. When's Independence Day?"

"May 20, 1898. That's when Cuba declared independence from the Spaniards, *los canallas.*"

"Spain?? Cuba??" His head quivered.

"Yes. Cuban colony declared independence from Spain in May 20, 1898. Then, we became a Russian colony in 1959."

"We didn't declare independence from Spain!" he informed her.

"No, we did. You were lucky. You had the British with their umbrellas and their silly tea cups."

Mister Apostolopoulos now felt clearly irritated. "Now, look! I don't want to know when Cuba declared its independence from Spain!"

"Eh? Then why did you ask me?"

"I didn't!" He took a deep breath, trying to calm himself down. "When did *the United States* declared its independence from *Great Britain*?"

The old lady bit her lower lip and looked to one side, thinking.

He waited.

"Now don't rush me," she warned him.

He waited some more.

"It was in July," he volunteered.

"Ah! The 14th of July."

"No . . . . That's the French holiday. Bastille Day."

"Ahhh, the French," she said as if remembering them after a long search. "You know, French people are pigs. Have you met any French people? Pigs! They're pigs! They're all pigs!"

"WhenisthedateofAmericanIndependence?" he shot out in frustration.

"That's what you should have asked me in the first place! Why didn't you ask that in e first place? July 4, 1776." Now, it was her turn to explode. *"¡Ay, pero este hombre no sabe hacer las preguntas!"*

Apostolopoulos took a deep breath for his last question. This question he always asked, no matter how short or long the interview, how pleasant or unpleasant. It was a fun question. "Ok, this is the last question . . . (thank God)" he added in a lower voice. "When was the War of 1812?"

The woman paused and thought about it, making a face as she thought. She thought some more, making a few gestures with her hand.

"The War . . . of 1812," he repeated.

Maria thought some more.

"The War . . . OF 1812."

"Now, don't rush me," she said waving him away.

This was the limit! He stood up, hands on the table, leaning forward. "The War . . . OF 1812!!"

"Was it in 1812?"

"Yes!" he exploded. "Yes! The War of 1812 took place in 1812! It's over!! You pass!! NEXT!!"

Maria was very happy, as was Olga, who entered the room and realized that her mother had passed the test, contrary to her expectations. They hugged and squealed with joy.

"Your turn now," he informed her and Maria left her daughter in the room, but not without patting her in encouragement.

"Ok, I'm ready!" Olga announced, barely containing herself.

"Good." He took a deep breath. He was going to start fresh. "All right! Let's start! Who was the first president of the United States of America?"

Olga smiled and answered rapidly, one word running into the other. "George Washington, a Virginia planter who, during the War of Independence, was the Commander in Chief of the Continental Army. During the early stages of the war, he avoided engaging the British forces because one defeat would've meant the annihilation of the Continental Army, which was stationed at Valley Forge. Later on, he went on to victories. He was tall and distinguished and handsome. He was married to Martha, they had no children, although he regarded Alexander Hamilton as the son he never had. As an old man, he wore false wooden teeth. During his administration, he was painfully aware that he was setting precedent as first president, so he was careful in everything he did or-"

"Ok! Enough!" he interrupted. "Who wrote the Declaration of Independence?"

Again, Olga shot out the information. "Thomas Jefferson, another Virginian planter, as tall as Washington, but with red hair. He was also an architect and a naturalist. Earlier, he had written political essays, including *A Summary View of the Rights of British America.* The Declaration itself was presented before the Continental congress whose members proceeded to amend it in countless ways. As the third president of the United States, Jefferson's most memorable achievement was the purchase of the Louisiana Territory around the Mississippi River from Napoleon Bonaparte, who had acquired it from Spain. It effectively doubled the size of the United States. He subsequently launched an exploration of the new territory expedition, headed by-"

"Ok, Ok! Enough! Next question: when was the War of 1812?"

Olga did not spit out the answer. In fact, she said nothing, just stared at him for a few moments.

"What?" she finally asked.

"When was the War of 1812?"

She stared some more.

"You gotta be kidding me!"

"Nope. When was it?"

She looked momentarily to one side, frowning.

"I know it's not a trick question . . . . What, you think I'm stupid?" she asked him, a bit insulted. "What kind of a dummy is going to miss this question?"

Apostolopoulos just answered with a wicked chuckle.

"1812!" she finally answered.

"Right! Congratulations! You passed the exam."

"That's it?? That's all?" She was clearly disappointed at not being given the opportunity to shine.

"Yep. It's obvious that you know the material." He made a face now. "That and the previous exam took longer that it was supposed to."

"Wait a minute! I've been reading up for weeks on this! I pulled an all-nighter for this!

"No need!" He began to gather up his papers and stood up.

She also stood up.

"But, we barely scratched the 1700s! and you didn't ask about the early colonial period, the 1600s! We barely touched the 1800s."

Ignoring her, he began to turn to leave, but Olga went around the table to face him.

"And what about the Civil War, that's when things really get interesting! Robert E. Lee. Abraham Lincoln."

He motioned with his arm for her to get away as he sidestepped her.

"What about Teddy Roosevelt? He was a fun president! You skipped the entire 20th century, the Depression, Woodrow Wilson and his Fourteen Points."

Apostolopoulos made a dash for the door, only to have the girl block his way, still talking.

"What happened to Pearl Harbor and World War II? Hey, 'I like Ike!' The first men on the moon were Neil Armstrong and Buzz Aldrin while Michael Collins was left along up there flying around the moon twiddling his thumbs, waiting for them to return. Ronald Reagan was the best president of the second half of the 20th century while Jimmy carter was a putz! John F Kennedy is the most overrated president in the history of-"

"Go away!!" was the shouted plea that was heard by the rest of the applicants outside, waiting for their turn.

ELENA

Because the commencement speaker at her graduation was droning on and on and on in a monotonous litany of clichés, like about how it was the graduate students' duty to be self-sacrificing and unselfish, to put one's own wellbeing and wishes to help The Poor, the Glorious Poor, without actually saying why, exactly, did The Sacred Poor deserve it, what The Sacred Cow Poor had done to actually merit this special treatment, that Elena's mind began to wander. Her daydreaming, though at first random, very soon came to follow a sequence of events in her life. As absurd as it may sound, she had not really sat down and followed these events in her life in any ordered, logical manner, not really. On her behalf it must be said that while going to the university she had overburdened herself with additional projects and reading materials, far above the basic requirements for each class.

Many years ago when, for the first time in her life, she was suddenly confronted with bleeding, she was naturally terrified, all the more so as her mother had never given her any advance warning. Not unreasonably, she thought that her life was in danger, that she would bleed to death. Fortunately, for her, it happened while she was in her back yard, atop the tree house that her father had built for her and in which she went to for solitude, so that social embarrassment---the phobia of every female since the dawn of time---did not take place.

She climbed down and ran inside her home

seeking her mother. But, once her mother learned what had occurred with a gasp, she shoved her bewildered daughter into the bathroom, threw a handful of sanitary pads in Elena's face and slammed the door behind her.

When her father came home, exhausted from work, a couple of hours later and had settled in, he asked his wife, "Where's Elena? She's awfully quiet."

"She's in her room. She won't come out."

"Oh-oh. What happened?"

"She got The Curse today. She came in screaming and crying, thought she was dying."

"How did you handle it?"

"What do you mean, how did I handle it? I took her to the bathroom and gave her some sanitary pads."

The father gave a low growl of annoyance and got up from his favorite chair, where he had comfortably settled in and went to his daughter's room. He knocked at the closed door.

"Elena?"

"Elena, can I come in? It's Dad."

No answer.

"All right, well, I'm coming in." He did so. She was sitting by the side of the bed, looking down. He sat next to her and put his arm around her shoulder. "Hey, now! Mom told me what happened today. Congratulations."

"Congratulations?" she glanced at him, the back down, not sure that she had heard right.

"Yes, congratulations! Today you're a woman! So, come on, we're going out to celebrate."

"I don't want to, daddy. I'm not in the mood."

"But I am. We're going to a restaurant, Red

Lobster, your favorite. We'll stop by '21' and pick you up a new dress and then we'll finish it off with a movie. Come on!"

It took a little persuading, but she went along. She knew that he was trying to cheer her up and would have resisted out of spite, except she *did* like eating at Red Lobster and she *did* want a new dress and she *did* want to see Brad Pitt's new film. Besides, he had called it a celebration and . . . hey, maybe it was that, after all.

Only her mother objected because she had made dinner. Meatloaf.

"Put it in the fridge. We'll have it tomorrow. It's not every day that our daughter becomes a woman."

By the end of the night, Elena's misery was a vague memory.

-      -   -   -   -   -   -
       -      -   -   -   -

It cannot be said that Elena and her mother were on good terms.

Quite the contrary.

Elena chafed at the constant restrictions imposed on her life, no, on her happiness, by her mother.

"Don't sit like that. Good girls don't sit like that."

"Don't laugh so loud! Ladies don't laugh out loud. It's vulgar. Cover your mouth!"

"Don't run like a boy!"

"Don't horseplay! You're not a boy!"

Predictably, she began to, first, envy boys, their freedom and their bodies, then to hate them for the same reasons. It did not occur to her that, like so many other countless girls before her, she was misplacing her anger.

"Stop reading so much and come into the kitchen and learn how to cook. Someday you'll have to cook for your husband." It was only the fact that her father periodically kicked her mother out of the kitchen when he was in one of his frequent cooking moods that prevented her from altogether hating to cook. In fact, a couple of times when he was in the kitchen, she asked him to teach her how to cook some of his specialties, which he did grudgingly, as if he was imparting a secret.

Elena's mother seemed to be firmly guided by two principles in regards to her daughter. The first was that Elena's sole destiny was to get married, to find a husband, and the sooner the better; it should be her only interest in life, her only goal. The second was really more of an almost Japanese-like preoccupation than a principle: what will people think? To this end, she sought every opportunity to psychologically hamstring her daughter---though she certainly did not see it that way, no, on the contrary, she was simply taming an unruly spirit. For her own good, you understand.

Again, Elena misplaced her anger into hating men.

One time her mother went too far.

"Stop reading so many books. Men don't like a girl who's smart."

Her husband overheard her and leapt out of his chair as he threw at her the glass of tea that he had been drinking, missing her face by inches and screaming insults at his wife at the top of his voice.

"Don't you EVER tell her to stop studying! Don't you EVER tell her to be stupid!!" This while holding a trembling clenched fist in front of his wife's face. Not for the first time did Elena realize just how big her father was.

A demarcation line formed. Her mother could nag her about cleaning and cooking---but school was off limit. Crossing the line would result in World War III in that family. Even when Elena went out for sports at school, with her father's enthusiastic encouragement, Elena's mother kept quiet, though her face spoke volumes.

Her father, in the meantime, would brag to anyone, at the slightest excuse, about how smart she was, about her being third in her whole school (it sometimes seemed to his listeners that the connection between his daughter and the topic at hand was a slim one). She was especially adept at mathematics, even mastering calculus, a subject that had always befuddled him and this in itself practically made him drunk with pride.

For her seventeenth birthday, he had bought her a microscope. For her eighteenth, he had bought her a telescope.

-    -   -   -   -   -   -
-    -   -   -   -

There was one night that Elena and her father had an important conversation. They had traveled outside the city, away from light pollution, to an empty field with fireflies flicking on and off, where they had set up the telescope to watch Jupiter and its moons now that the planet was close to Earth.

Her mother had been particularly overbearing recently and Elena's bitterness was bubbling over, yet what came out was a diatribe against men. She was repelled and disgusted by men, their boasting, their aggressiveness, their horse playing, their strength, their rowdiness, and their masculinity.

"Really, Elena," he father had reproached her. "Men are not the enemy. Haven't you figured out by now who the enemy really is?"

This threw her into momentary confusion in suspecting that maybe there was something there that she had overlooked, something that was apparently obvious. But it was just momentary.

"What about wife beaters, Daddy? What about those men that want wives that are idiots, that don't know anything?"

"Honey, I'll grant you that there are some men out there who have an inferiority complex. They're morons. They're neurotic. Scum. Yeah. You just gotta avoid them like the plague. They're poison. But, to think that all men are like that, well, that's just dumb."

"See, a woman who's really smart, really educated, or who has a better paying job, now that's something to brag about. She's a *prize*. She's a source for bragging."

"But, Daddy, men have all the advantages," she went on. "It's a man's world. Women don't have any opportunities at all, all roads are closed to them."

"I'm surprised at you, Elena!" he responded angrily. "A girl of your intelligence saying something so stupid! Men and women each have their strengths and weaknesses, their advantages and their disadvantages. If you think that men have it easy in this world, I wish you could turn into one to see what idiocy your spewing out. I've never heard you before talk this stupid! Really, Elena! And I thought that you were intelligent!" He spoke with anger, contempt and disgust in his voice, the first time that he had talked this way to her.

It was one of the few times as a young woman that her father had reprimanded her and the fact that he had called her stupid---which he had *never* done before---felt like she had been kicked in the stomach by a mule. In the darkness, she hid her tears.

It was much, much later that night, as they now viewed Mars, the Pleiades and the moon that Elena suddenly asked him, impulsively, without any forethought. "Daddy, why did you marry Mom?" His first wife had been a geologist, killed in a car accident by a drunken Mexican.

The question took him by surprise for a second. He then smiled and kissed her on the forehead.

"Because of you, honey."

She frowned, puzzled by the answer, then her eyes got as big as saucers.

The night viewing had come to an end. On the way back to their car, her father quietly told her, "It's my earnest hope that you don't turn out like your mother."

-    -   -   -   -   -   -
     -    -   -   -   -

She went on to the university, of course. Her mother consoled herself with the idea that at least there she would find a suitable husband, a future professional. Her idea of a college degree was not a BA or BS or an MA, but a Mrs.

In the first year of college, she dated a young man with a goatee. She unburdened herself to him and he was sympathetic. Then she got the feeling that he wanted her to realize how broadminded *he* was by dating an intelligent girl and that she should feel grateful. His self-confidence was shaken after he told her, with pride, that he was a Marxist. He was wearing his favorite Che Guevara T-shirt.

"Really?" Her eyebrows arched in mild surprise and stared at him for a couple of seconds before speaking again. "You're always saying how progressive you are and here you are advocating a doctrine that's almost two centuries old. That is actually being reactionary. Especially for a doctrine that's been shown to be intellectually bankrupt again and again, resulting in mass starvation, censorship, concentration camps and repression, no matter who, or where in the world, it's applied."

Being a good Marxist, the young man could not tolerate anyone who disagreed with him and saw her no more. Elena shrugged it off.

"Elena Canales!"

She abruptly woke up from her daydreaming on hearing her name called out and she marched up to the stage and took her diploma as it was handed to her. As she came down, her father took a picture of her with his camera. If anyone could possibly look like he could explode with pride, it was he. Come to think of it, so did her fiancée, a surgeon, standing next to him also taking pictures of her with her diploma.

FLAPJACKS FOR THE SOW

The nine year old boy deplaned at the Miami airport and joined the line of other Cuban refugees, mostly adults, crossing the tarmac and entering the airport building. An uncle and aunt were supposed to meet him there, his parents had told him, but he did not know what they looked like.

The arrival was a tumultuous scene, Cubans naturally given to hysterics no matter what the occasion.

"Luisito!" a man called out to him, waving, then came over, very excited and hugged him.

The boy correctly assumed that this man was his uncle.

At first, he did not notice the fat woman that accompanied his uncle and who regarded him with mixed emotions, until she spoke with him.

Unknown to him and to his parents his arrival was not totally welcomed. When his father had asked the uncle to pick him up at the airport and care for him until he and the mother could escape (and this was communicated in the most highly veiled language that could pass by the Communist spies that were the long distance operators in Cuba), the fat woman had objected once the telephone conversation had ended. An argument had ensued.

"I don't want that brat here! Let him go somewhere else!"

"Let the Catholic church put him up! They've been doing it with all the kids that are being sent over!"

"That's for the children who don't have

families here! I'm the boy's uncle and you're his aunt!"

"I don't care! Tell them not to send him until his parents come over with him!"

"Woman, are you nuts? You know that it's catch as catch can! They were lucky to get the government's permission to take him out! The Communists want especially the kids for brainwashing!"

"I still don't want him here! Let him wait a little longer!"

"They can't take the risk! They might not get another chance and, besides, the kid's dangerous. The Communists are busy brainwashing the children to turn in their parents if they say anything the least bit against the regime!"

The shouting match ultimately ended without the boy's family being any wiser.

They picked up the boy's one small suitcase, the only thing that he had been allowed to leave with by the petty minded gangsters who believed that another suitcase containing toys or comic books would bankrupt their precious Revolution.

Once in the car, Luis' uncle began to pump him for information about the situation in Cuba. Luisito poured it all out, having repressed it for so long and he told them about the scarcity of food and comic books, the *stupid* Soviet films, the Russian cans of food which caused botulism, the neighborhood meddling spies, the fanatics, the enforced militarism. He went on and on.

They arrived and he was shown to his room. After a few days, they became accustomed to each other. The boy began to slowly become accustomed to little things in the new culture. One of his favorite foods turned out to be pancakes, or flapjacks, although in the very beginning, anything that was put in front of him was devoured, as they stared wide-eyed at him eat.

Ordinarily, this famished cleaning of the plates would have gladdened any woman's heart. Not so with his fat aunt.

One night, about two weeks after his arrival, he sat up in bed, smelling the unmistakable smell of hotcakes. He got up and, in his brand new pajamas that his uncle had bought for him, followed the smell to the dining room, where his obese aunt was seated, slowly eating pancakes (his uncle was out of town on business).

"What do you want?"

"Oh . . . ah . . . I just wanted a glass of water," he replied, somewhat shy.

"Oh, yeah? Sit down, I'll get it for you." The boy sat at the opposite end of the table, hungrily eyeing the pancakes and the glass of water was set in front of him. He sipped it, meekly, while she resumed eating her food with a smirk, all the while eyeing him.

The boy sat quietly, expectantly, while she finished her food. She got up and put the dishes in the sink, the ten pound roll of fat beneath each arm swaying from elbow to armpit.

"All right, now go to bed," she said with a malicious grin on her face, as she wiped off the syrup from her mustache with her fat arm. The boy did so, confused about what had just happened. He did not understand why he had not been asked if he wanted some, according to Cuban hospitality. At home, even with the severe scarcity of food, one always offered food to someone who had dropped by while one was eating. He went to bed hungry, the smell still lingering in the air.

She, on the other hand, thought that it had been a very funny incident and that she had been rather clever and later recounted it to all her friends, oblivious to the odd looks that they gave her. She even told his parents when they arrived months later. They, for their part, smiled politely, grateful for their having taken care of their son. Years later, she still remembered the incident and could tell the anecdote with a smile on her face, and still did not notice the odd looks that her listeners gave her.

The boy would for years also remember the incident into manhood, though without any humor whatsoever and in later years, when speaking about her, invariably referred to the woman not by her name, or "aunt," but as *la puerca,* the sow.

Now a man, Luis obtained a well-paying job back in Miami, where he and his parents had gone to visit from time to time. He was glad to be back somewhere where the Cuban culture still flourished and was prevalent. He bought a house, insisting that the house have a basement because of the tornadoes that he had indirectly experienced while in Oklahoma. He furnished his new home in very good taste and his parents flew down a couple of times to visit.

One day, he came across his old, fat aunt and casually asked her if she could come and help him make up his mind about some furniture that he had put in his home for which he was not sure whether it suited the home or no. Not having much to do, she agreed to do so and got in his car. On the way over, they spoke about this, that and the other.

"It's this way," he said, leading her down to the basement. It was an ample basement, well carpeted and seemed to be like a regular room in the house. It had another doorway into another specious room, which, in turn, led to another room. "Just like our basement in Oklahoma. You could hide six families in there."

"Where's the furniture?"

"Over there," he motioned to the last room.

She entered it and heard the door lock behind her. She tried to open it, confused, then called out to Luis. He did not respond, even when she yelled to him. She looked around. It was a bare room with concrete walls; a toilet bowl was in a corner hidden by a walled partition. She was confused and became afraid.

She spent the whole day trying to get out of there and realized that it was impossible to do so and that Luis would not open it.

Hours later, she heard him come back, but he would not answer her. She then smelled smoke, metallic smoke, and heard metallic noises. She was scared out of her wits.

On the third day, having heard nothing or eaten anything in the interim, she heard the door click and she went towards it and was able to open it. She saw that a metal bars now enclosed the door, like a cage. On the opposite side of the cage, Luis was sitting on a chair in front of a table. He was wearing the plastic ear coverings worn by workers in very noisy workplaces. In front of him was a stack of flapjacks, over which he poured hot maple syrup. He ate leisurely, without looking at her.

Her aunt called out to him and motioned to him, but he ignored her. She kept on talking and pleading and shouting throughout his meal.

He finished his breakfast and calmly picked up his plate and left the room.

Once she calmed down, she realized that she was still unable to get out of her predicament. Also, the smell of the food lingered and made her hunger worse.

Cubans can be wonderfully vindictive. They have been known to wait for years for retribution.

Luis came back from work that evening to have his dinner downstairs. This time it was *arroz con pollo*. His aunt stared at the food and asked him to at least let her have some food to eat. He left after finishing his meal, taking the plate with him. Before doing so, he picked up a grain of tasty rice and threw it at her. She picked it up and put it in her mouth. There was just enough taste in the grain of rice to be tasted and it was just enough to make her hunger more acute.

Next morning, he breakfasted with bacon and buttered toast and drank coffee.

The smell was maddening.

This torture went on for days and days. Not once did he look at her, or address a word to her; he would eat in front of her everything that was tantalizing with its aroma, from pizza to steak.

Because of her accumulated fat, it took his aunt weeks before she finally died of starvation.

It was then that he removed the bars and the emaciated body and disposed of them both.

APOLOGY ACCEPTED

As was his habit, Ray Robinson had risen early, earlier than his family, and was working on some figures on the dining room table. He liked to say that it was this time of the day that his mind was clearest and at its best. By now, it was eight o'clock on a Saturday and his family would be beginning to stir before too long, with the kids making a beeline for the TV for the weekly ritual of Saturday morning cartoons.

He sat back, sighing. No matter how he worked and reworked the figures there was no way around it, he had known the conclusion beforehand. He had hoped, nevertheless, that some new, unforeseen solution would simply pop into his head, but it all added to the same conclusion: if he did not acquire $150,000 within three weeks, his business, an eight year concern, would fold.

A month ago, he had overextended himself in order to fulfill a huge order that had been placed with his store, which would have yielded enough profit with which to start a second store across town, something that he had planned on for some time. He had delivered the merchandise just in time for the recipient to file for bankruptcy. As a result of the bankruptcy petition, Robinson could neither recover the merchandise nor could he collect on the billing. The most that he could recover was ten cents on the dollar, an attorney assured him with an artificial air of commiseration, while his opposite number assured the recipient of the bankruptcy with a genuine air of shrewd appreciation.

And it was all perfectly legal! As legal a case of legalized theft as alimony, or eternally escalating taxes for the benefit of professional welfare recipients, or nationalization of industries by Socialist countries.

When he learned of this, and further learned that his inventory was absurdly low and would need to be replenished, Ray Robinson had his wife immediately sell the handgun that he kept at home for fear that in a moment of weakness, he would use it injudiciously.

Now, as he put his empty cup of coffee in the sink alongside the dish containing toast and butter crumbs, he was certain that a bank would extend a loan with which to replenish his inventory. The drain on him on the coming years for repaying the loan, though, would be a heavy burden. He had also read somewhere that money was tight now, so he might have to apply to several banks.

The pitter-patter of little feet was soon followed by a "click" and then the voice of Bugs Bunny. He smiled and went outside the house and into the garage.

The lawn needed mowing, so he would mow the lawn in the morning before the afternoon heat. He would not do so before ten, however, since it was a Saturday and his neighbors might be sleeping in late. No sense in waking them up with the noise, he thought, so until then, he would file the blades or maybe change the spark plug and the oil filter. He began to putter around the opened garage.

A Rolls Royce slowly drove up the street and hesitantly parked on the kerb opposite Robinson's house. The man driving peered out, as if looking for an address, then got out of the car, again in a hesitant manner. He was dressed impeccably in a three-piece suit and sporting a derby. In some people a derby looks plain silly. On this particular individual, it accented his good taste in expensive clothes.

To Ray's surprise, the man began to approach his house. Ray leisurely exited the garage, first making sure to wipe his hands clean on an available cloth. As he slowly approached, the man in the hat looked at him, then at his cupped hand and then repeated the motion, whereupon he placed his hand in his suit pocket, apparently putting away something.

"Are you Mister Robinson? Ray Robinson?"

"Yes, I am. Can I help you?"

"How are you this fine morning? I'm glad that I caught you up and about, instead of waking you."

"Yes, I was getting ready to fix up the lawnmower before cutting the grass," he said, looking around at the lawn. "It's getting a bit high." He chuckled. The grass was actually very high.

There followed an awkward pause. "And you are . . . ?"

"Oh, sorry. Terrible manners. Delgado. Manuel Delgado." They shook hands.

"And what can I do for you?"

The man looked embarrassed. "Well, this may sound a bit absurd. In fact, I *know* it does. Especially since it comes clear out of the blue. Didn't you go to Public School #427 in Union City around 1964?"

Ray chuckled in surprise. "Yes, I did. As a matter of fact I did. Sixth and Seventh grade, I think. Did you attend there?" He now became mystified.

"I was a classmate of yours," said Delgado.

From his breast pocket he removed a folded paper, which, when he unfolded it, was a copy of a class picture. He pointed to one of the distinct pictures, that of an eleven year old boy smiling. "That's me."

Robinson remembered the class picture well and he frowned. His mother had torn their copy in anger. Altogether, it had been a miserable year and his family had moved away, this time to Trenton. As a boy, Ray had had problems in that school at that time and he had been miserable.

It had started with the influx of Cuban immigrants into the surrounding neighborhood. They had arrived like locusts. Where once there had been quiet, clean secluded streets---a good neighborhood, very cute---now there was trash on the sidewalks, loud voices constantly shouting to each other across the street, rude and ill-mannered men and women, and louts hanging around in groups uttering lewd remarks to passing women. Of all their distasteful habits, the most repulsive was the continual, obsessive spitting. One could hardly pass a Cuban without hearing the rasping noise as the throat was scraped of a sticky glob, followed by a loud expulsion of green, white, or yellow glob of phlegm flying through the air until it finally landed. Worse, it got so bad that one could not navigate the sidewalk on Bergenline Avenue in a straight line without stepping on the repulsive evidence that a Cuban had recently passed. Even after a rain shower, the outline of the corrosive glob was still discernible. He remembered it being impossible to navigate the sidewalk without stepping onto those sticky globules that dotted the pavement. It was enough to make anyone gag with revulsion. In this, they were just like the Chinese. In the schools throughout the area, a similar deterioration had occurred.

The Cubans seemed to arrogantly reject the fact that they were guests in this country and behaved abominably.

Upon looking up, he was surprised to see Delgado's face troubled, then he realized that Delgado had reacted to his own obvious stress, probably written on his face, when Ray had been shown the class photograph. He tried to be less tense.

"Quite frankly, I vaguely remember you at all," he said quietly.

"Do you, then, remember *him?*" Delgado asked, pointing at a wolfish-looking boy.

"Yes, I do. I certainly do," he said with obvious distaste. "José was his name, José something."

""I didn't like him, either, quite frankly." Delgado said. "A typical loudmouth Cuban boy."

"Excuse me, but I seem to remember you being Cuban as well. And you do have an accent."

"Yes, I'm Cuban." He paused. "This may sound odd. Let's just say that there are a number of . . . traits found in us Cubans that, in an overall sense, fill me with disgust. The way that they raise their children is top on my list." He paused and looked away briefly.

"Do you remember the last day of the school year, we were told by Mrs. Granger to bring games to the class party? Do you remember that a pack of kids followed you after school, jeering? For no particular reason? That, as you ran, while surrounded, you tried to protect your game? That José led the pack? That he broke and scattered your game? That you were scared and hurt and you were crying? That you felt terrorized? Well, I was one of those little animals and I've never forgotten the look on your face."

Ray remembered well the incident. All that Delgado had said had indeed happened. He had arrived home sobbing his heart out to his mother who had tried to comfort him as well as she could, even though her own heart was livid with anger and pain and hate. It was shortly after this incident that his father had decided to move out of the deteriorating neighborhood for a healthier one, even if he had to commute to work. The sheer, sadistic cruelty that he had experienced had haunted the boy for years and the reason for it had evaded him, even though the truth of the matter was that there had been no cause, no reason for it.

"I know that, ordinarily, excuses would be made that we were 'just kids,' or that it happened so many years ago," the older Manuel was saying to him, "but I don't accept such excuses when it comes to children suffering, even when the suffering is caused by other kids." He shifted uneasily. "Look, I know that this sounds as crazy as anything, but I've tracked you down after all these years to apologize to you. I am truly sorry for what happened. The cruelty was simply despicable and I have been sorry to have been a part of it."

As Ray listened dumbfounded, it suddenly occurred to him that to this man, the incident had weighed on him as much as it had on him. For him to remember, after all these years *and* motivate him to search Ray out just simply to apologize to him, must mean that he had been as pained by the hounding as he himself had been as the victim. All these years! It must have been eating away at his conscience. He began to wonder about the man's sanity. Ray extended a hand, forcing a smile.

"Apology accepted," he said as they shook hands. "You're a remarkable man, Mister Delgado, to do this. Would you like to come in and have some coffee?"

"No, I must be going. I have some errands to attend, but I do thank you. Besides, my presence is a reminder to you of that painful incident." He looked around and shifted his feet.

"My trip here has a more practical purpose. As a way to make amends, I would like for you to have this." He removed an envelope from his breast pocket and extended it to Ray, who just as he thought that he had recovered from a surprise, now had to deal with another.

Inside the envelope was the title to a Rolls Royce and a cashier's check for $250,000. He looked up at Delgado and his mouth opened and closed several times, like a fish out of water. Delgado took Ray's hand, turned it palm up, and plopped car keys on it and pointed to the car across the street. He smiled. He was now obviously immensely enjoying this part.

"But, but," sputtered Robinson, "this doesn't happen in real life. This is too much!"

"Not to me, it isn't," Delgado said, "this country's been good to me."

"But when . . . but when that incident happened, it was José, it was that José who did it. He was the culprit, the instigator. You didn't do anything. I remember. I remember it clearly."

Delgado became serious again.

"Exactly. *I didn't do anything.*"

He let the words sink in before continuing. His voice now had a formal tone, as if lecturing. "At one point or another, many of us have done something, or, conversely, not done something, that resulted in the suffering of an undeserving Christian soul. Well, such is the case with me, except that, unlike most of those persons I am in a position to make amends. I can rectify the wrong as best I can, even though I cannot erase the pain that I may have caused, directly or indirectly, or the particular incident."

He paused again for quite some time, while the one man audience stood stock still. He repeated himself. Apparently, he had given this matter considerable thought.

"At one time or another, each and every one of us has done something shameful that has caused immeasurable pain on another being. It may have been intentional, or accidental, or unthinkingly. Or, it may have been *not* doing something that should have been done. But, unlike most people, I have the means to make amends. I know that it may be impossible to erase the wrong, but I can create an equivalent, or greater, amount of good."

"Well! I must be going!" He shook hands again with a stupefied Robinson. "And thank you for accepting my apology. Goodbye!"

"Goodbye," answered Ray, feeling like he was in a dream. The keys and the envelope in his hand were real, however. He vaguely wondered if the check was a legitimate one. Maybe it was a practical joke.

The man in the derby hat went to the curb and looked down the street and gently motioned with his hand. A limousine slowly drove up, apparently having been there, unnoticed all this while. As it did so, Mister Delgado felt as if a weight had lifted off his shoulders. He got in and waved goodbye to his former schoolmate, who was still in a daze.

The man next to the chauffeur turned around to speak with him.

"Everything went OK, Mister Delgado?" he asked in a very respectful voice.

Delgado looked up at the private detective that he had hired to track down Ray Robinson's whereabouts and smiled. "Yes, it did. I feel very good about it. I dare say that that money will come in handy."

"It's all in the report I gave you. He got ripped off not too long ago for $150,000. Did you bring it up?"

"No, that I didn't," he replied. "If there's one thing that I've learned about Americans is that they are fanatical about their privacy. He might have gotten even more upset about that than about losing his business." He sighed. "Well, that's one chapter that I can close behind me." He arched his neck and stretched. "Who's next?"

The private investigator lifted three folders and chose one.

"Of the three, this one lives closest."

Delgado looked at the name and recognized it with a twinge of pain.

"Have preparations been made?" he asked his hireling.

"It's all in the report," he replied. "We should arrive in two, maybe three hours," he said looking at his watch.

Delgado sighed. He relaxed as he alternated between reading the report and watching the scenery roll by. Hours he could spare. Days he could spare. Weeks he could not. The cancer that he was harboring in his body was spreading too fast.

"That's the good thing about knowing that you're about to die," he thought. "It forces you to take stock of your life."

THE COLLABORATORS

Oftentimes have I heard you speak of one who
commits a wrong as though he were not one of
you, but a stranger unto you and an intruder
upon your world.
But as I say that even as the holy and the
righteous cannot rise beyond the highest which is
in each of you,
So the wicked and the weak cannot fall lower
than the lowest which is in you also.
Kahlil Gibran, *The Prophet*

Four men sat inside a breezy porch, talking
amongst themselves, on a warm Cuban night, the air
strongly scented by honeysuckle. They were
engaged in the Cuban national pastime of laughing
at others' misfortunes. Since the events that they
were discussing were ones that they coincidentally
benefited from, there was quite a bit of gloating as
well, since it dovetailed perfectly with the unstated
precept by which all Cuban men and women lived
by, which was, "stab your fellow man in the back
and laugh about it afterwards."
The four men were brothers and they,
naturally, visited each other on a regular basis.
Tonight, they met at Arsenio's home in Marianao, a
Havana suburb. As was the custom, they sat apart
from the women, who were talking about topics that
could only possibly interest them. One of the
brothers was Miguel, a farmer whose *finca* was near

the border with Matanzas; he was not present in the frequent gatherings as often as the other brothers because of the distance. This time he had come to La Habana in order to go with his brothers to look over the display of brand new farming equipment that the new revolutionary government was going to distribute to the farmers as part of The Agrarian Reform. It goes without saying that no one questioned how, or who, was paying for this beneficence.

They had returned an hour ago from the open air exhibition. Although it had been much ballyhooed by the government and droves of people had gone to gawk at the various brand new tractors, mold boards, rakes, cultivators and disc plows, Miguel could tell that few of the passersby (city folk) were actually really enthusiastic by the display, being outside their field of interest. They had turned out just out of curiosity. Nonetheless, he himself had been impressed and was now anxiously anticipating the delivery.

The revolutionary government had also decreed, through The Agrarian Reform, that henceforth, farms would be restricted in size to thirty *caballerias* (a thousand acres). The idea had been around for many years, the implied argument being that no one should have too much land, but the real reasoning could more honestly have been voiced thusly: "since I can't have that much, nobody else can." Needless to say that no one questioned by what right could one mob, or government, or committee, dictate to an individual how much land, or money, or cars, or clothes, or jewelry, or books, or neckties, that individual could own.

As a result of the decree, Miguel's neighbor,

for example, Frank Martinez, would lose nearly half of his farm, the "excess" then being distributed to Those Less Fortunate. That Martinez and his family owned the land fair and square, that they had worked all their lives like plow horses from sunup to sundown, that they proudly loved their farm, that it was one of the most efficient, best run, farms in the region, that they had bought neglected and untilled land and had busted their backs turning said land into fruitful agricultural *caballerias,* and, more importantly, that they did not want to sell, was deliberately left unmentioned. Not that it would have made any difference. With a mixture of envy and greed, like circling vultures, Martinez's neighbors waited, wringing their hands in anticipation for the "redistribution of wealth" to occur, already making mental calculations as to how much of the booty they would each be able to grab.

Miguel was one of these neighbors. For years he had cultivated for bananas and tobacco in his ten caballerias, but it seemed that he was more proficient in harvesting tarantulas and bats than anything else. He was telling his brothers how much he expected to receive, what kind of land it was and his plans for that land, and as he did so, and his brothers offered suggestions, he could not help gloating over the anticipated acquisition.

"But isn't that stealing?" a small voice asked during a lull.

The men were stunned and a brief silence ensued.

The question had been asked, in all innocence, by Maximito, Esteban's ten year old son, who had been silently following the conversation throughout without saying a word, just listening and watching. The other children, as usual, had initially also followed the adults' conversation, but had earlier dispersed to play in the street and were now buying pirulí from a passing vendor. In his straightforward question and his staring eyes, little Max had stirred the broken, mutilated vestiges of what had once been a conscience within the adults. Because of this, he was instantly, momentarily disliked. Fortunately, his father came to the rescue of everyone.

"No, son, because, you see, the government is going to compensate the owner by buying up the excess land. So, he'll get money for his land. What a question!"

This was true, there would be compensation for the confiscated land. Little Max was relieved, being too small to see through this fatuous argument. The adults could have done so if they had given any further thought to Martinez's viewpoint, but likewise accepted the compensation explanation, satisfied at not having to dwell on an unpleasant topic and perhaps even revive and been forced to come to terms with their long-stunted conscience.

"Now, go play with the other kids, son."

"But I want to stay and listen."

"This is grownup talk. Go!" And little Max joined the other children and was soon happily busy playing ball with his cousins. The adults were relieved to see him go, although the gloating stayed subdued as a result of little Max's question.

Earlier in the year, a similar incident had occurred. The government had suddenly decreed that those families who lived in a rented home, or a rented apartment, now owned that dwelling and did not have to pay rent, since it was now theirs. This declaration increased the popularity of the government. Since Esteban had been for years renting his home at a reasonable rent from a retired Polishwoman living next door, he was overjoyed at the announcement and even became insolent towards her whenever they crossed paths. The Polishwoman emigrated soon afterwards, damning Cubans to hell, having seen the handwriting on the wall, selling her own home in the process; she had had only one house to rent, having worked in painstaking frugality for over a decade in order to pay for her investment.

Soon, thereafter, the brothers had come together to visit and this was, naturally, a topic of conversation, or rather, gloating. Agustin, the third brother, had also been renting his home, so the amount of gloating can only be imagined.

At that time, little Max had, once again, with that untarnished sense of right and wrong that so many children all over the world are born with before their parents crush it out of existence with either scorn, cynicism, or justification, shattered the mood with his question, "But, Daddy, isn't that wrong?"

And, of course, there was nothing that one could have answered to that too innocent question, because it *was* wrong, it *was* unquestionably immoral, it *was* very wrong and this time there hadn't even been an anesthetic-like excuse of "compensation" because no compensation had even been contemplated anyway and the stark reality was there for all to see: that the drooling Cuban population, under the guise of politics, was taking turns in preying upon one another, tearing each other to pieces, without the slightest hesitation, or shame, on the part of those receiving a share of the spoils. In a certain sense, the fact that this victimizing of others who were better off was being done under the justification of an overglorified international political doctrine of rationalized cannibalism was merely . . . incidental.

So, the father had responded in the only way that an adult Cuban felt was appropriate.

"What a question! And what do you mean by interrupting the conversation of adults? You're just a child! What do you know? Go and play with the rest of the kids!"

So he did. And it was a good thing that the boy had no idea of what buying items (cars, refrigerators, furniture, etc.) on the installment plan was all about, because the government then decreed that The People no longer had to make further payments on whatever items that they had bought on the installment plan and could go ahead and keep the items, said customers ending up with those items at a fraction of their cost.

By the end of the year, the subsequent confiscation of all American businesses, invariably described as "exploiting Yankee monopolies" and "colonialist footholds" were an accomplished fact and, of course, most of the country chuckled with approval. An abstract anti-Yankee feeling was a long-standing tradition of Cuban life and, in fact, of *all* Latin American political life, which to this day has been often utilized by dictators of the entire political spectrum, from the left and from the right, to either mask their illegal actions behind a show of hysterical chauvinism, or, in order to take attention away from their own crimes. From long practice, dictators throughout Latin America of the entire political spectrum knew that they could always count favorably on an otherwise pointless show of anti-"Yankee imperialism" gorillaesque breast beating. The Latin American masses---and *especially* the intellectuals---always responded automatically and favorably to this ploy, just like Pavlov's dogs salivated at the ring of a bell and with just as much mindlessness, the same mindlessness for which Latin Americans are so justifiably famous the world over.

*   *   *

*   *   *

The Communists desperately played for time. Each day, they consolidated their hold on the country that much more. On the one hand, they had to allay the fears of the Colossus of the North---only ninety miles away---who was, after all, the primary opponent of Soviet expansionism and would, undoubtedly, invoke the Monroe Doctrine as soon as their suspicions were confirmed of The Revolution having turned Marxist. They would certainly not tolerate a Russian beachhead in the Americas! On the other hand, the Communists had to systematically, yet surreptitiously, pacify or liquidate those revolutionaries whose original ideal had been to get rid of the dictator Batista and his murderous henchmen, like the vicious Mansferrer, in order to reestablish a republic. The Communist clique had to replace them with their own Marxist henchmen, particularly in key positions, or turn as many of them into Communists as was possible. Even more daunting, they had to downplay the obvious Communist makeup of many of their followers and their policies and continue to ride the wave of overwhelming enthusiastic support that had been present because of Batista's overthrow. It was a formidable, unenviable task. It was a real tight wire act.

Many of the original rebels who complained of Communists being placed in key positions, particularly Communists who had not lifted a finger to overthrow Batista and who, in fact, had supported the dictator right up to the end, actually blamed Raul and the psychotic Che and assured themselves that as soon as Fidel learned of the problem, he would take the proper steps---unaware that he himself was the Prime Mover in the events taking place. When they finally came to the realization of how matters really stood at, it was too late. The Trojan Horse was inside the gates and its contents had discharged.

Baseball in Cuba, as in Japan, Santo Domingo and the United States, was a national mania. A glimpse of Fidel Castro's mentality occurred when, months after having seized power, he appeared in a Havana stadium as a batter for one of the national baseball teams and was struck out. He immediately declared that it took four outs to strike out a batter. The pitcher and the umpire, being nobody's fool, instantly agreed and the pitcher then pitched a ball which could have been hit by a teenager. The Cubans altogether missed the significance of what had happened and, instead, thought it was a funny, quirky episode. Castro was happy; he had proven his proficiency in baseball for the whole world to see and admire; at that time, no one knew that years prior he had traveled to America to play in one of the national baseball teams and had been rejected, hence his rabid hatred of Americans. That particular incident should have right away sent up a red flag of warning and set people to thinking, but, as we all know, Cubans find thinking---accompanied by silence---to be a distasteful, painful activity and dutifully avoid it whenever possible.

The international Communist conspiracy rallied to their colleagues' defense. A torrent of articles, petitions, newscasts, films, demonstrations, documentaries, declarations by ad-hoc political--- and supposedly nonpolitical--- groups appeared praising the Cuban revolution, the newly acquired benefits to The People, and pointed to the grass roots support of The Revolution, and condemned American "paranoia," which was obviously based on "McCarthyism" and was going to end up sending Cuba into the arms of the Soviet Union if American pressure did not let up, and which demonstrated America's colonialist outlook towards its southern neighbors. Legions of protoCommunists, with their hyena grins, tripped over themselves in a stampede from all over the globe towards Cuba in a pilgrimage, all for the privilege of meeting the Maximum Leader and then groveling at his feet and also give The Revolution (always spoken in capital letters) their own particular seal of approval. Some, like C. W. Mills and Jean Paul Sartre even published tracts gushing their enthusiasm and lambasting the United States. They spoke not a word of Spanish. No matter.

*　　　　*　　　　*　　　　*
　*　　　　*　　　　*

Let us look closer at the brothers.

A short man, prematurely balding, Agustin

was a civil servant whose specialty was sports, that is, the representation of Cuba in the international arena through sports, a position which, although unknown in the United States, is common in many countries. Such a position has many perks, foremost being paid travel to other countries. When Batista had been in power, he had been a fervent Batistiano and sang Batista's praises. Upon hearing of Batista's overthrow he had been the first in his street block to sport the red and black armband with the yellow "26" in the middle of it. He genuinely welcomed and applauded the revolution and the anticipation of a return to democracy. At the present, he denounced "Yankee imperialism" and the counterrevolutionary "caterpillars" along with the best of them and could outshout anyone in the open air mass meetings with the preferred slogan, *"Patria o Muerte! Venceremos!"*

Nor was this hypocrisy. On the contrary! Each time he had been sincere. He was simply an unconscious chameleon. Had the United States Marines landed instead of the American government adopting a pusillanimous policy towards Castro, I dare say that he would have been singing *Yankee Doodle* at the top of his lungs in the Malecon. Curiously, far from being seen as unreliable by the Party, his star was rising rapidly within his bureaucracy and was actually even being deemed as above suspicion and allowed to travel abroad without fear of defection, or espionage.

Arsenio, the eldest brother, was a high school principal. He had earlier been a teacher, but was now a principal in a new State school which had formerly been a school run by the Catholic church and had been confiscated by the State. Since the overthrow of Machado in the Thirties, he had been a closet Marxist; that decade had been a turbulent period in the nation when college students had actually, briefly, for all practical purposes, run the country and debates as to which ideology to follow (National Socialism, Fascism, Socialism, Communism, Anarchism, maybe something new and vague and purely Cuban) had never gained a consensus and public debates were oftentimes resolved with bullets. Many concepts in Marxist ideology had always appealed to him, both the stated ones and the implied, and he had promoted those ideas and debated them with his colleagues and his brothers, though he had never joined The Party. As such, he was what is known as a "fellow traveler." In recent months he had refrained from formally joining The Party and declaring himself a Marxist-Leninist at the request of The Party: the time was not ripe. Soon. Very soon. In the meantime, he continued to promote government proclamations and advocated vigilance in the schools and elsewhere for the safeguarding of The Revolution. Children were to extol the virtues of Fidel, Raul, Che, Russia and, of course, The Revolution itself, and they were to notify their teachers at once if they overheard their parents making any derogatory remarks on the new icons. In their turn, teachers were ordered to report any counterrevolutionary statement blurted out by any of their pupils. The G-2 would then "investigate" (if he had known just how many of his teachers risked their necks by *not* reporting such occurrences, he would have had a fit of apoplexy).

He personally conducted tours of visiting foreigners---sympathizers of The Revolution, of course---as they toured the "new, improved" educational system, so that they could return to their own countries and rave to one and all about the benefits to The People in Cuba. As they followed Arsenio with their perpetual hyena grins, they made mental notes of the proven benefits. And they did so uncritically, although usually and with all other topics in their own countries they were invariably cynical, sarcastic and suspicious. Had Arsenio casually informed them that, as a result of The Revolution and the new educational system, six year old children could easily carry out quadratic equations in their heads and recite *War and Peace* word for word, from beginning to end, and in the original Russian, the visitors would have uncritically accepted such claims and, what's more, would have returned to their respective countries and testified to such an achievement. And if any of them noticed the children toting submachine guns and being dressed and drilled in a decidedly militaristic fashion as potential cannon fodder for Fidel, Raul, Che and The Party against the "imminent" Yankee invasion, none ever commented on it---even though at home they were caustic in their stance against their own country's military---especially if it belonged in NATO. They certainly did not condemn the fact that Cuba had, overnight, become the most militarized State in Latin America.

In his own block, Arsenio had formed one of the first "neighborhood committees" for safeguarding The Revolution, whose task it was to spy on his neighbors in that block, report conversations as well as comings and goings to the G-2, speculate as to any possible counterrevolutionary "caterpillars" infesting the block, organize "spontaneous" demonstrations and marches of contempt against the increasingly longer queue of those seeking a visa in order to emigrate, and assure attendance and support to the open air rallies where Fidel would hysterically rant and rave against the Americans, practically foaming at the mouth for four or five hours at a stretch, in Hitler-like fashion. He also had first pickings in looting any homes of their personal belongings deserted by emigrating "counterrevolutionaries" in his block and could even move in to the vacated homes if so desired (or move in a friend or relative) and if it was a step up in the quality of his domicile.

Needless to say that he was intoxicated with all this new power that he wielded. He was living the dream of every 19th and 20th century intellectual.

The odd man out was Esteban. As the months passed, his disillusionment was steadily increasing. It was not that he objected *per se* to the anti-Americanism of the new government, nor to The Agrarian Reform, nor to the closure of the fifty-eight independent newspapers and magazines which were replaced by only one, nor to the persecution of the Catholic church, nor even to the pro-Russian propaganda. Being Cuban, he could easily disregard others' persecution, suffering and deprivation. Rather, it was that he objected to the natural, inevitable byproducts of a decrepit Marxist economy, where guns, not butter, and where both quantity and quantity of basic consumer goods had flown out the window. In other words, he himself was being adversely affected. Again: the detrimental end result of Marxism-Leninism was affecting him and his family directly. Suddenly, there was no soap, razor blades, or deodorant; no shirts, pants, shoes, dresses, belts; one had to line up for hours to get *one* can of condensed milk, or *one* can of coffee, or tuna, or pears, or rice, or milk (while chanting moronic pro-government slogans!); medical equipment, medicine and drugs had disappeared; nobody could find a television, radio, fan, record player, much less a car, for blood or money; bookstores became empty; decent entertainment became nonexistent; travel was restricted; all tools like flashlights, pliers, batteries, nails, hammers, resistors, gone; even *sugar, tobacco,* or *Bacardi rum* had vanished---in Cuba! In Cuba! He could not remember the last time that he had had a Cuba Libre, or his children a *guarapo* drink from sugar cane---in Cuba, for God's sake!

This was a novel experience. It had *never, ever* occurred before in Cuba. Not with Batista. Not with Machado. Not even during the Great Depression. It was unheard of!

So this was Communism.

On the other hand, his brothers, in their enthusiasm, did not object to the adverse shortages because their rewards for unquestioned obedience outweighed any shortages that they had to endure and which would, "of course, be temporary."

And another thing: the politics likewise affected him directly---even though he had no interest in politics and certainly had no political ambitions. Heretofore, with the Machado and Batista dictatorships the government simply left you alone. True, they had been a national disgrace. They had looted the country. They were sadistic thugs. Yet, the implicit rule had always been that as long as you did not take any part in attempting to dislodge the regime, you had absolutely nothing to fear from the regime's killers. This was a rigidly enforced rule. Iron clad. But, if you planted bombs, hid a *cache* of weapons, hid conspirators in your home, well, then, all bets were off and you had to take the consequences. People began to mutter to their family that Batista may have been scum, no argument there, but at least you could eat, have food, go to a movie, or a bookstore, or a nightclub. Besides, if you did not mess with him, he really did not mess with you.

It then came as a shock that this new, *totalitarian* regime did not want to leave you alone, did not believe in privacy, that instead it saw nonparticipating neutrals with as big a fear and hate as the active "counterrevolutionaries." This new paranoid regime wanted your endorsement, your participation, your loyalty, your enthusiasm, your *soul.* So . . . all independent sources of information, education and entertainment were taken over and regimented for the purpose of ensuring that the whole country responded as with one mind, one voice, one mindless voice: endless adulation of The Revolution, Che, Fidel, Raul, Red China, the Soviet Union; everyone was equal; the Yankees were the Great Satan, the source of all evil, what the Jews had been to the Nazis; the rich had to be persecuted and robbed; militarism for the glory of The Party and The Revolution was noble. And so on, *ad nauseam.*

And it was this constant intrusion at work, at home (through the radio and television), at his neighborhood (with the Neighborhood Committees spy network), his children's school and the insistent demands for participation that both angered and intimidated Esteban and his family.

They-would-simply-not-leave-them-alone.

They even had to stifle their complaints about the recurrent shortages. And since it was never certain whether the next door neighbor, or the colleague at work, might be an informer, inhibition

149

of speech became necessary. When one takes into account what the Cuban national character had been up to that time, which was to engage in endless verbal diarrhea (universally acknowledged, by the way), one can immediately sense that the situation was becoming intolerable.

The Communists had achieved what had hitherto no one had thought possible: they had made the Cubans finally shut up.

Which goes to show that every black cloud has a silver lining.

As for Esteban.

While Esteban suffered from this type of stress, his other brothers felt little, if any, discomfort. Agustin was busy wholeheartedly being a chameleon, while Arsenio endorsed everything that Esteban found intolerable. As to Miguel, he was too busy in the fields away from the capital to be bothered with much and, besides, the new cooperative was about to be formed soon.

Now, as to what Esteban did for a living. He worked as a physician, a doctor, in a hospital, making a modest, but comfortable, living, enjoying the respect that is everywhere accorded a physician (just as his brother, Arsenio, had with being a teacher).

*　　　*　　　*　　　*
　　*　　　*　　　*

At the present time, Esteban, Agustin and Arsenio had returned to where Esteban lived in the Miramar suburb after having attended an exhibition of Soviet Russia's scientific exploits. It had attracted a large crowd because it included film clips of Gagarin, the first man in space and so, even "cowering counterrevolutionaries" had gone with curiosity and anticipation. The exhibition was a mixed success, however, because there had also been film clips of Leika, the first dog that had been shot out to space and another of a dog whose head had been amputated and successfully grafted onto another dog, now having two heads, and had lived for many hours. These two clips were a mistake and had caused subdued indignation since Cubans--- although having an innate talent---indeed, a gusto--- for tormenting helpless, inoffensive persons---they paradoxically hate to see animals abused and become very angry when they see an animal being cruelly mistreated (human beings, again, now, that is a different matter, that is Ok, that is enjoyable) . Inevitably, the exhibition had also shown film clips of the fiasco of the attempted space shots of American rockets humiliatingly exploding, toppling over, careening out of control, again and again.

Anyway, the brothers were now in Esteban's home and, as usual, there was the customary talk between them. However, lately there had been a noticeable change in the proceedings with Esteban on one side and Arsenio and Agustin on the other, arguing politics and ending in angry exchanges, though still within brotherly restraints. Up to now, it had been an opportunity for Esteban to blow off steam.

"*Y que?*" So? What did you think of the whole exhibition, Esteban?" Arsenio prompted.

"It was good! But I wish that they had shown more about the flight into space. How I would have loved to have seen that!"

"I wonder what it's like out there?" mused

Agustin.

"Certainly different," said Esteban.

"Without doubt, a dangerous environment. Full of risks. Extremes of heat and cold. No air. Nothing."

"I can't even begin to imagine it," confessed Agustin.

"Nor I," said Esteban.

"A major achievement for the human race by the Soviets," Arsenio probed.

"Without doubt," Esteban agreed.

"So wouldn't you agree now that the Russians, and Communism in general, are the wave of the future?"

"I just hope that humanity doesn't drown in this 'wave of the future,'" he retorted.

"There you go again! And what makes you say something so stupid? After what you've just seen?"

"Well, *chico,* when I hear Communists, I get the impression that they wouldn't have any hesitation at all in treating the whole human race like that poor Leika bitch and shoot it out to space just to see what it'd be like."

"So what the hell does that mean? Now, you're talking just for the sake of talking."

"Nothing. I guess nothing. I just don't like that Communist mentality that everything and everyone is expendable. I was browsing last night through *Darkness at Noon,* one of the few copies left in the country; that Hungarian fellow practically says the same thing."

"Fellow should have been liquidated long ago and all his books burned," murmured Arsenio.

"See? See? That's what I mean! That's just what I mean: 'Think like I do, or I'll kill you.' What kind of an attitude is that, Arsenio? It's not healthy! It's not normal!"

"It certainly wouldn't be healthy for the Hungarian," Agustin piped in.

"Yeah, well, it's that 'attitude,' as you call it, that made the Soviet Union what it is today-"

"I can't argue with that," Esteban muttered.

"-and that country's in the forefront of every human achievement. That's why I've decided to send Luisito to study there when he gets older."

"To Russia?"

"When did you decide that?" asked Agustin.

"A week ago."

"*Chico,* he'll freeze! Russia's in the North Pole. That's where Napoleon' army froze. And, besides, Luisito doesn't even speak Russian. And he certainly can't read and understand those chicken scratches that they make."

Castro was sending Cuban children to the Soviet Union in droves so they could be properly indoctrinated away from their parents and whether the parents wanted to, or not. Their numbers were reaching into the thousands. The Communists had also floated the idea of taking all the children away from their parents to be raised by the government in barracks. As an alternative, many desperate Cuban parents were sending their children to the United States, whether or not there was someone at the end to take care of them, and uncertain when, and if, they would ever see their children again, to the point that the numbers were 200 children a week. And those were the lucky ones

"Oh, he'll learn first. We'll have him learn Russian first before he goes. But, like I was saying, Communism represents the progress of humanity."

Esteban blurted out an obscenity to indicate

what he thought of that statement, then went on. *"Chico,* you're confusing Communism with Russia. The Chinks got Communism long ago and I don't hear of any space shots coming out of there. Nor the Koreans. Or the Poles. I don't know how it is in Russia, all I know is what I'm seeing right here with my own eyes and my eyes tell me that Communism is garbage! There's no food, no clothes, no cars-"

"Bourgeois desires," he sneered.

"Pah! It's bourgeois. So it's bourgeois. All right, call me 'bourgeois' and say I got 'bourgeois desires.' So what? Why can't life be comfortable and pleasant? Bourgeois! And is it 'bourgeois' to want to eat, or is starvation one of your Communist virtues?"

"This is temporary! Soon, the Russians will be helping us out and they'll be shipping you what you want so you'll be happy then!"

"Oh, so they're 'bourgeois' too, eh?" Esteban jeered and Arsenio boiled at having neatly fallen in the trap.

"And let me tell you something about that Russian foreign aid: I've had over fourteen cases of botulism in the hospital and each one has been caused by a can of that stinking Russian food! That never happened before! Have you opened one of their tins and smelled it? *Dios mio!* The food's spoiled! And *that's* what they're sending us? And have you seen their films? They make no sense! They're rubbish! The theaters are empty! Nowadays, you put on a film from Hollywood and there's a line going around the block four times over!" This was true and it was a sore point with the Cuban Communists.

"At least we're no longer an American colony! You with your precious Hollywood, you don't seem to know what's really important! You can't see the big picture and realize what's truly important! You give up Gagarin's achievement for the chance to see a film with Marylin Monroe, or Sophia Loren!"

"Pah! Ah, *chico,* I don't know about being an American colony, but there was certainly plenty to eat! Nobody seemed to contract botulism, or was starving to death, and let me tell you something else, with all these palefaced Russians I see running around here, I wonder if *we're* not becoming a Russian colony!"

"You are a traitor! The Yankees controlled our economy, our foreign policy! We didn't even. . . ."

And so it went, each time getting more and more heated, arguing the only way Cubans argue, which is with a lot of screaming, arm waving, insults and making noises and faces when "responding" to an argument, with Agustin being less forceful.

But tonight was somehow different. It was not the usual argument between the brothers. There was an underlying snarl to Arsenio's voice, an unspoken threat, particularly whenever Esteban would make one of his infuriatingly sarcastic comments. Agustin picked it up right away and was frowning at where the argument was going and the particular insults that Arsenio was using, while Esteban also felt it, but he was not conscious of it until the argument got so heated that Arsenio came right out with it.

"The Revolution can't afford to have traitors like you in the rearguard sabotaging The Party! We can't have counterrevolutionaries like you hanging around, ready to welcome back the Americans!

Wise up, or you'll end up liquidated---like Trotsky with a pickax through the skull! And it'll be good riddance, too!! You aren't just in the way! You're undermining The Revolution, the best thing that's happened to this country, with your seditious treason! The only way to shut you up is in front of a *paredon* firing squad!!"

The shouting ceased and the color drained from Esteban's face. Even Agustin, who had up to now agreed with everything that Arsenio had said, had blanched to the point that he looked like a Russian.

Finally, Esteban spoke and the calmness in his Cuban voice was eerie. "And would you pull the trigger . . . brother?"

"Don't 'brother' me! I'm a Marxist-Leninist and I don't go in for bourgeois sentimentalities! If you're going to call me anything, call me 'comrade.'"

Another pause in the argument.

Agustin then tried, awkwardly, to defuse the situation. He said to Esteban, "You said that it was the Russians and not Communism that was responsible for the advances, but it's not true. The East Germans have begun training our athletes and I predict that before too long, we'll walk away from the Olympics with a handful of gold medals."

His mind still preoccupied, Esteban nevertheless calmly replied, "Germans. *Chico,* the Germans are not Germans for nothing. Anything they do, they do well. Always. East Germans, or West Germans, North Germans or South Germans."

Agustin nonetheless went on, describing the training regimen, again trying to diffuse the tension.

Finally, it was time to leave and the visit broke up, Agustin and Esteban worried, while

Arsenio fumed.

Immediately after they left the house, Esteban quietly asked his wife, "Did Kiki ever agree to put up the poster?"

"No," she replied, "he said that they were out of them, but he was lying, of course."

Esteban nodded.

Kiki, the head of the local Neighborhood Committee, had pasted one of those unbelievably asinine posters that Marxists are so fond of, extolling one moronic thing or another, in the garage door of every house where he felt the occupants were one hundred percent behind The Revolution. About three houses in the street did not have one and one of these was their home.

That night, Esteban came to the decision to go into *el exilio,* to leave the country. She agreed.

It took months of arduous and humiliating lining up for visas and passports and making the right contacts but, slowly, one by one, the members of the family left the country carrying just one suitcase of clothes, to be reunited at a later date. When the last family member left, Kiki had his favorite cousin move into the vacated, furnished home.

It was a very nice, very comfortable home, nicely furnished too. It even had two air conditioners. The new occupants had something new to be thankful to The Revolution for. Months later, they would meet a French intellectual to whom they would tell that The Revolution had given them a furnished home; the intellectual would assume that the home was created from nothing, out of thin air, by the regime and had he known whose home it originally was, he still would not have cared and would have still praised The Revolution,

Communism, Fidel and his minions.

*   *   *   *
    *   *   *

It was now in the open. Fidel Castro, in one of his five hour megalomaniacal speeches, announced to the world that he was, and had always been, a Communist. By this time, the takeover had been successfully completed, against all odds.

And not only that, but the anticipated invasion at Giron Beach had been repulsed and the United States thoroughly humiliated. In one of the most incompetently carried out operations in the annals of military history, Cuban refugees had been openly recruited in Florida and trained in the jungles of Honduras by Americans (the Cubans had immediately began to bicker amongst themselves, naturally). Everything that could possibly go wrong with a military operation went wrong. The American President---possibly the most overrated president in the history of the United States---had been halfhearted in the effort.

Then, in 1965, two speeches opened the floodgates of refugees. Castro proclaimed that anyone who was not satisfied with The Revolution could leave the country. He had been urged to do so by his Russian colonial overseers who had profited from their lessons during the 1956 Hungarian Uprising: after the revolt, they had not sealed the borders into Austria and had thereby created a pressure valve. No more uprisings occurred in Hungary. Cuba was an island and too far away for Russia to send in its famous tanks to crush any successful uprising.

The second speech came from the American President Johnson at the base of the Statue of Liberty as a response to Castro's speech: all Cuban refugees would be welcomed into the United States.

Like most dictators and all fanatics, Fidel Castro was unhinged and refused to accept what did not accord to his delusions and preconceptions. In short, he had believed in his own propaganda. The most that he expected to leave were a few hundred. When thousands scrambled to leave, he was infuriated and had to be persuaded from ordering his troops to machine gun the lot.

*   *   *   *
     *   *

By this time, Esteban and his family had established themselves in their adoptive country. At first, it had been very hard because of the language barrier, the culture shock, the homesickness and the lack of a comparable job. But, they adjusted, always thinking that "next year" they would be back. Other Cuban families were encountered and they began to reach out to each other. Americans were very sympathetic and tried to help out, all but the American intellectuals, who desperately pined for a similar catastrophe to descend on their own country.

The doctor had not given up on his profession (unlike many other professionals who emigrated) and had worked his way up past the foreign language efficiency test, the residency and the unbelievable State Board Exams.

He had just passed the Florida Board and

was celebrating in his Pensacola home with other Cuban doctors and their families. The phone rang and he answered it, a Cuba Libre in his hand.

"Esteban?" a voice asked. "It's Esteban? It's Miguel!"

"Miguel! Where the devil are you?" Telephone calls could not go out of Cuba, only incoming calls and it had been a long time since they had spoken. The family quickly crowded around the telephone and the others quieted down, also excited by the news.

"In Opa-Locka, some place called Opa-Locka, in Florida."

"Florida? You mean, you're here? It's Miguel! He's in Florida! When did you come over? God! What a surprise! I had no idea! When did you come over? Is Maria with you?"

"Two days ago, *chico*. Some people here tracked you down. We told them your name and what city you lived in and they found your telephone number."

"Listen! We're on our way down! When can you get out? I mean, where they got you?"

"We can leave any time. Soon as you get here, in fact."

"Ave Maria! What a surprise! We've got lots to talk about . . . !"

That afternoon, the whole family packed into the car and drove down to Opa-Locka.

Once there, amidst a profusion of hugs and kisses and "You look just the same!" and "My word, he's grown!" Miguel and Maria were crammed into the car and headed towards Pensacola. Miguel recounted their passage out of Cuba. Then, the family began to reminisce and, for some reason, Maria recounted the time that she had climbed a tree to get some fruit at their finca and stumbled against a wasp nest and the wasps had covered her face.

Miguel recounted how bad things had become in Cuba, with all the shortages and the constant political meetings. But what really brought out his indignation was how he, for all practical purposes, had lost control of his *finca* once the cooperative finally got running and all sorts of interlopers stuck their noses in his business and he had to lend out his farming equipment, which was usually returned damaged, or unclean, and how he had been forced to allow others to live in his *finca* . . . ."

Throughout the trip, "little Max" (he was not so little anymore) just stared at them without saying much, unless he was addressed directly, much as he would stare at some curious insect. On several occasions, Miguel caught Maximito looking at him with that look that he had often seen in the boy's face, years back in Havana when the brothers used to get together and talk.

After all these years, that look still made him uncomfortable.

*　　　*　　　*　　　*

*　　　*　　　*

Meanwhile, very little changed in Cuba. Things just became more so.

After his secret, enforced hospitalization in a mental hospital for paranoid hallucinations, Che Guevara left and infiltrated Bolivia in order to spread The Revolution. When the Bolivian peasants failed to idolize him and follow him, he brutalized them. Hunted down and killed, his severed hands were secreted out of the country to Cuba, where Castro displayed them in a museum as medieval holy relics. Guevara's sayings urging death and destruction in every direction were posted throughout Cuba and his likeness was reproduced in billboards, airports, stamps, busts and whole sides of buildings. He was shown with flowing hair and Lenin-like Tartar eyes staring off into the distance dreamily envisioning whole countries aflame. That image was copied and adopted by legions of protoCommunists in the West from Sweden to America to Chile.

For a while, there was even hope in Havana that the United States (and for that matter, Italy, France and West Germany) would experience a similar Revolution. The activities of thousands of "peace activists" carrying Viet Cong flags and posters of Mao, Che and Ho were followed closely in Havana as they tried to shut down Chicago, Washington D. C. and other American cities. Bombs were set off by New Left (Communist) groups called the SDS, the Weathermen, the Yippies, the Black Panthers. Some of the wannabe "revolutionaries" even went to Cuba. The American mass media, for its part, lent itself one hundred percent behind the movement, helping to create a climate ripe for a leftist totalitarian takeover. Yet, somehow, inexplicably, The Revolution in the United States never materialized and the wannabes missed their rendezvous with history and faded into anonymity. The closest that they came was in the 1972 election with George McGovern when they hijacked the Democratic Party and its rank and file members, shocked at their tactics and their arrogance, deserted *en masse* and actively campaigned for the Republican Party.

Whereupon the wannabe revolutionaries did not simply disappear, but instead blended into the woodwork of universities and the mass media, where they would, for the next decade voice their admiration for Cuba, Vietnam, the People's Republic of China and the Cultural Revolution and snarl about the rich being too rich and powerful in the United States, while simultaneously suppressing any views which were not Politically Correct, using a plethora of tried and true tactics.

But Cuba itself remained the same. Only more so.

*　　　　*　　　　*　　　　*
　　*　　　　*　　　　*

Maximiliano, a young man now and attending college, opened the door at the request of his father, in answer to a persistent doorbell. Juan García and his wife, Rosa, stood at the entrance. Max stifled a groan and a thought flashed through his head, "Ten years in this country and these idiots *still* haven't learned to call ahead, they just drop in!"

"*Ah, hola!*" he greeted them, forcing a smile of welcome. The niceties of Cuban hospitality had to be observed.

"*Hey, que pasa?*" We were in the neighborhood and we thought that we'd drop by and see what you guys were up to."

"Come in," Max was forced to say. "Everyone's here. We just finished a late lunch," and he announced the visitors, who entered the den where the rest of the family was at, including Uncle Miguel and Aunt Maria. Additional chairs were brought out and conversation continued as if Juan and Rosa had been there from the start.

Max stayed with them for about a minute out of lethargy and then went to his room. He ordinarily took part in conversations now that he was an adult, but only if the topic interested him. He still made the others nervous, but this time with his relentlessly caustic comments and too truthful observations. In truth, he also had the same effect on those leftists that he mercilessly raked over the coals in college, completely unafraid of the repercussions. He puttered in his room and picked up a book that he had been unbelievably lucky to find, against all odds, entitled *Fall of a Titan* which he had almost finished (like all books---very few books!---critical of Communism written in the 1950s and 1960s, it had been successfully relegated to oblivion, unread, uncited, unreferenced). He put it off for later and instead mused about possibly going to the shopping mall.

He went to the kitchen to get a Coca-Cola. Nothing of what drifted over from the den aroused his interest. He noticed on the kitchen counter a mailing from an exile political organization; in the flyer there were several pictures of the organization's officers and their fat wives in Europe, posing like tourists before famous landmarks. The bulletin stated how much lecturing about Cuba's problems the officers had undertaken while in Europe. There was no question whatsoever in Max's mind that all of their expenses---including their wives'---were being paid through the contributions of its members. All of their faces reflected that brazen shamelessness that is so typically Cuban.

Then, Max heard the faint hollow metal sound of the mailbox being closed and went to get the mail that the postman had just deposited. In reviewing the mail, he saw a small envelope of dismal quality with a stamp portraying the psychotic Che Guevara. In reading the return address, his eyebrows shot up. He opened the letter and read the contents.

He came into the house.

"Any mail?" asked his mother.

He handed the letter over to his father to whom it was addressed and said, "You're not going to believe this."

Esteban took the letter. "It's from Arsenio!" This caused a stir. He read it silently, then smiled. "He's coming! He's applying to emigrate!"

"No!" exclaimed his wife.

"When's he coming?" asked Maria.

"Just him or his wife?" Miguel inquired.

"Run out of victims, has he?" This from Max, with a smirk.

"Does he say when?"

"No, he doesn't know when it'll be, but he writes that he has made the decision for certain."

Max snorted. "I suppose he's expecting a welcoming applause."

"It's obvious that he can't say much, because he's afraid that the letter will be read. He's not going to put down his reason why."

"You know," said Maria, "I always thought that it'd be Agustin who'd come over first."

"Me too," Miguel agreed.

"You do?" Max quickly jumped in. "*I* don't. We've got a librarian in the college who was also a lifelong Communist and came over three years ago and he's always apologizing, or bragging, I can't tell which, about having been blind to 'reality' all these years as a Communist and how Communism is the pits. My guess is that the famous 'Party discipline' finally got to Arsenio."

They had no idea of what he was talking about.

But Esteban agreed with Maria. "I have to admit, I also thought that it'd be Agustin to be the one to get fed up."

"Why?" asked Max.

"Because deep down, he's a plain opportunist. Always has been."

"All the more reason why you're wrong!" he countered. "Don't you get it?"

Nobody did. They shook their heads and looked at each other, perplexed.

"Reason it out. Agustin is an opportunist, but Arsenio's a lifelong Communist intellectual thirsting for power, the pestilence of the twentieth century. All right, at first there's plenty of victims and lots of spoils, so all the cannibals benefit from the cannibalism, whether they are Communist, or not. It's all very Cuban. But, sooner or later, the victims run out. After all, there's just so many rich that you can feast off of. So, you fall on another group and devour them and redistribute the spoils. Now, of course, every once in a while, you have individuals who don't belong to the current group of victims that's being victimized at the moment and they either flee the country, or they get shot, and *their* goods get split up. Problem is, the quality of these goods is getting shabbier and shabbier as the years pass and as they get handed around, and the number of available victims gets fewer and fewer."

"Well, Arsenio is a good Party member and has to follow 'Party discipline,' which means mindless obedience and sacrifices for a future good. By now he's gotten jaded with his power, but the Party makes more and more demands of him. Basically, he's now just a flunky! A flunky who has run out of victims and of spoils."

"Agustin, on the other hand, makes frequent international trips with his sports teams. Buys a lot of first class foreign goods: clothes, food, books, televisions, records, you name it. He's doing fine. *And,* his area of expertise has high priority with the regime because they want lots of medals from the Olympics because they think that that legitimizes their regime."

"It's not that the Communist countries are that interested in sports *per se.* They feel that an excellence in international sports mirrors the 'excellence' of their repressive, regimented society and eclipses its shortcomings---the lack of food, the lack of freedom, the lack of travel. And it's true. In a way, they're right. It works through a kind of 'desensitization' and you stop to think of them solely in terms of secret police and the Berlin Wall. Besides, they think that if their athletes beat the athletes from capitalist countries, that means that their political ideology is better. And that is why Agustin will always be in clover."

"Makes sense," his father said. He had never stopped to think about it in any depth.

"And it fits with Arsenio coming over," said Miguel.

There was a pause, then García spoke up. "What did you mean it was all very Cuban?" Miguel and Esteban quickly glanced at each other worriedly. They were used to Max's abrasive viewpoint, but García had never been exposed to them. And Maximiliano could get so caustic when he got carried away in an argument.

"In a nutshell? That we deserve what we got," he acidly replied.

"What?"

"Just what I said: that we deserve *exactly* what we got."

"Well, explain that, I'm not a mind reader," he snapped back, already beginning to feel irritated, inexplicably so since Max had not been overly caustic. It was just that there was something about him . . . .

"Look, it's simple! We all keep referring to 'them' and 'the Communists.' All of us! But the truth is that the fault lies with *us*. It's really us, don't you see? *We* welcomed the revolution, *we* followed Fidel, *we* became anti-American, *we* did what we were told and *we* victimized others. Not 'them.' *Us*. But now we deny it and we've made ourselves forget that nasty little fact and we make out like we're the victims."

"Look, it's like this: the Germans, the Poles, the Hungarians, the Lithuanians---they had no choice! *They were invaded!* But we don't have that excuse. That's a luxury that we simply don't have."

"The famous Russian tanks went through Hungary and Czechoslovakia and Latvia and Poland. In those countries, their soldiers were slaughtered, their national monuments were blown up, their women were raped, their books were burnt in bonfires, their industries were dismantled and carted away to Russia and then the Russians told them, 'Congratulations! You have just been liberated by the Red Army!' But we don't have that excuse, that luxury. We did it ourselves---to ourselves! A Russian didn't put a gun to our heads and told us to chant, 'Cuba sí! Yankee no!' We volunteered to do so. Be honest, now. Come on! And when we started to steal from each other and denounce each other to the regime, that was doing what came natural to us."

"No! There I can't agree with you!" García finally put in. "When that *cabrón,* Batista, was overthrown, it wasn't to set up Communism! The original revolution was subverted. We were going to do away with the evils that plagued Cuba."

"Yes! Yes!" Max joined in. "Absolutely! One hundred percent! I agree with you one hundred percent. The thing is that the original revolution was going to do away with those evils in Cuban society, but those perceived evils were only skin deep. They were going to cure the symptoms, but not the disease. The evils that were reflected in society were really the evils within the Cuban character--- and there *is* such a thing as a national character. There is! *You* all talk about the American character all the time. Well, if you'll be honest with yourselves for five minutes and think back, you'll admit that when the Communists started their shenanigans, it dovetailed perfectly with our national character: the propensity to lie for the sake of lying, stealing from someone whenever the chance offered itself, taking advantage of those who were harmless and could not protect themselves, ridiculing others, not respecting other people, incessantly talking badly about others. That is all part of the Cuban national character and that is why I say that we *deserve* what we got. We certainly can't blame anyone else. I mean . . . *who else is there to blame?"*

By now, everybody was interrupting and

shouting, "Not true!" No!" "You're exaggerating!" "You're just ashamed of being Cuban!" "It's not true!" "Where did you come up with such an idea?" He shouted right back and it was pandemonium.

At one point, after about fifteen minutes of chaos, he suddenly got quiet and calmly raised his hands, palm open, apparently asking for silence. After a while, he actually got it and he was finally able to speak in a normal voice.

"Let me ask you all one question, a simple question: who among you remember the Chinese in Cuba? I do, and I'm younger than all of you."

"OK. The *chino manila.* So what?"

"Thank you. You just made my point. *Chino manila.* We showed no respect towards them, we ridiculed them to their faces, we never called each man by his name, just 'chino manila.' And to an Oriental, respect is everything! How they must be laughing at us now! Frankly? I'm ashamed of how we treated them, especially when I see how decently the Americans have treated us, with our thick accents and all. And if you *really* want proof of everything that I've said, take note that *none* of you feel any remorse whatsoever."

Strange to say, this last argument half convinced his listeners (only temporarily, of course) although they muttered that he had still exaggerated.

Nevertheless, he, stupidly, mercilessly, went on. "And what about the times before Castro and the Communists? What about the corruption and thievery and the mutual victimization between neighbors? How are you going to blame that on Fidel? No. It's *us.*" Several heads were now nodding their heads in agreement. Two hours later they would forget everything.

Max gave a short laugh at a thought that

popped into his head.

"And I'll tell you what else. I'm going to make a prediction. OK, you've got Arsenio and you've got that librarian jerk who was also an ex-Communist. One of these days the whole Communist Party, and the whole G-2 is going to come over and complain that conditions in Cuba are intolerable. Hell! We might even get Raul, or Fidel himself." He laughed again. "And if we ever overthrow them, *nobody* is going to admit that they were a collaborator. *Everybody will have been a victim.* Of 'them.'"

"Listen. I study history. When the Nazis occupied France, the French collaborated with them wholeheartedly and helped them against the British and in tracking down Jews for the gas chambers, but when the Americans kicked out the Nazis for them, not a single collaborator could be found. They all claimed to have been in . . . '*Le Resistance.*' So they attacked some poor women who had dated German soldiers, shaved their heads and used them as their scapegoats. Why? Because the French are pigs. They've always been pigs. Well, I predict it's going to be the same way in Cuba. Suddenly, nobody's going to admit to having been a collaborator---not even the Communists."

This drew a chuckle from everybody and several offered their own predictions along the same line.

"Look, it's simple," Max returned to his theme. "If we don't admit it, how it all came about through our own fault and our role in it, nothing will ever change, even after Communism is overthrown. Nothing will have changed."

Several were nodding in agreement, saying, "Yeah, maybe he's got a point there." Two hours later they would forget everything.

Then, Esteban looked again at the letter and remarked, "I wish that I knew when he was coming. I suppose he can stay in the living room for a while, sleeping on the sofa bed."

"What? What did you say?" asked Max, wide-eyed.

His father repeated it.

Max spoke slowly.

"I can't believe you said that. I can't believe what I just heard with my own two ears. After all that he's done . . . ." He shook his head in disbelief.

"Well, *chico,* I don't care. He's still my brother."

"Bourgeois sentimentality," Max sneered and his father stiffened at the reminder.

Regardless, Arsenio was not able to leave for several years.

*   *   *   *
     *   *   *

And then, several years later, came the bizarre spectacle of the Peruvian embassy in Havana.

Castro, furious, since he had often stated that by that time most of those who could not stomach The Revolution had fled, proclaimed that whosoever was not happy with the incalculable benefits that The Revolution had brought to the nation could leave the country, at which point a mass stampede took place towards the embassy. A police cordon was thrown around the embassy. Even so, over ten thousand people made it in to the point that there was standing room only in the embassy grounds.

The Maximum Leader was not a happy man.

The Peruvian ambassador protested over the conditions and, finally, the port of Mariel was chosen as the departure point for this new wave of refugees, over one hundred thousand, who henceforth became known among the Cuban-Americans in Miami as the *Marielitos.*

Upon arriving in Florida, it was immediately noted that they were different from the previous refugees. They were not as vociferously anti-Communists as their predecessors and, in fact, revealed little of themselves, no doubt due to an acquired decades-long habit of not saying anything incriminating in a totalitarian society which would have dire results. Some people jokingly praised the Communists for having achieved the unthinkable---having been able to create Cubans who could actually keep their mouths shut.

There were also more blacks and more clue collar workers and more ex-Communists than before, people who had earlier seemed to have benefited from The Revolution and had themselves victimized others (quite a few of them were out and out criminals).

Among them were Arsenio and his family.

DRIFTING SEAWEED

Those who would sacrifice a generation to realize
an ideal are the enemies of mankind.
Eric Hoffer *The Passionate State of Mind*

If an airplane---a small one, not a jet
airliner---had been flying over that particular stretch
of the Caribbean, at that particular time of the day,
and, if neither the pilot nor the passenger(s) had
been drowsy from the uninterrupted, featureless
monotony of the scenery and the drone of the
motor, then they might have noticed in the distance
an infinitesimal speck on the surface, no larger than
the period at the end of this sentence. But the fact
was that there was no plane traversing the sky at
this moment and even if there had been no pilot
would alter course out of curiosity to see just
exactly what that dot was.

All around that dot was ocean, ocean, ocean.
Uninterrupted, endless ocean.

Clinging to that microscopic flotsam was
Roberto Romero, a young man (or an older boy,
depending on your viewpoint). That drifting,
directionless dot was a makeshift raft that he had
assembled out of three very worn out inner tubes
tied together with a rope which went through the
openings and through the holes that he had made in
a sheet of canvas.

It goes without saying that both the canvas,
the inner tubes and the rope were stolen. Cuba being

under the "benign" rule of the Communists, everything---*everything*---was virtually unobtainable. For a long time, longer than his own memory, everything had been unavailable, whether it was something mechanical and expensive like a television set, or an automobile, or something simple, like a decent pair of pants, or a brick, or a hammer, or a record. And, of course, the food. True, there *was* food---barely---rationed by a regime that boasted of having improved the standard of living of the country in its thirty year old iron grip. The upshot of the situation was in turning the Cuban people---who had never been too honest, anyway---into compulsive thieves.

Anyway, the sea was calm, as calm as it can be in the summer in the Caribbean. Even so, a wave would wash over him now and then. There were many white clouds, too, here and there, which passed between him and the sun. In fact, he had planned and waited for just such a cloudy day, which would minimize his exposure to the sun's rays.

He drifted.

The young man knew that the current, the mighty Gulf Stream, was taking him away, even if he could not tell that there was actual movement taking place; it was taking him from his native land and, should he have had a change of heart, he would not have been able to go back. If uninterrupted, he could actually end up in the Atlantic Ocean. Conceivably, there was even a very, very remote possibility of ending up in Bermuda or in Europe. Or perhaps even Iceland or the North Pole.

Hopefully not.

His hope was that he would end up in Florida. After all, Key West was only ninety miles away from Cuba. Or maybe even one of the many islands of the Bahamas. Just drift right on in, land in one of the beaches. Or, perhaps be picked up by a boat. Roberto had a hunch that there might be heavy traffic around these waters. He did not know, such elementary information being restricted by the regime, the same type of regime that in a European capital, a concrete wall had been erected around it to prevent its citizens from leaving repression, shooting anyone who dared to try.

Americans were all rich, he figured, they must have lots of boats to go out in and catch red snappers. Cubans, too, Cubans in Miami, that is. That's where his destination really lay.

Roberto clung to his tube, one of the three, that he laid on. From time to time, he arched his neck to look around. Nothing but water. He was certain that he was traveling, but because there was no point of reference, nothing solid, no rock, no island, no ship, there was really no way to tell and he was bored.

He tried not to think about his mother. She would be worried once she found the letter and read it. She would have surely found it by now.

He had tried to explain---how could he?--- yet she knew. That feeling of suffocation, of hopelessness, that feeling of being fed up, that there has to be a better life, that one is not an insect to be grounded into the dirt for one's entire life by the all-powerful members of the Communist Party, who, to add salt to the wound, had the shamelessness to claim---no, boast--- that the people supported them for their benevolent acts.

Once in Miami, he would write her, or call her---that sounded so unreal---and let her know that he had made it and was safe.

He wondered if learning English was hard. Some said it was easy, that it was full of words with only one and two syllables.

He had his regular clothes on, soaked by now, of course, and he checked one pocket. The sandwich was still there, sealed in a plastic bag that had been used and reused and washed and rewashed for so long that it was on the point of being worn out, so thin had it become. There was a thermos, too, older than him and rusted, with fresh water, tied to the rope by the cup's handle. He had a canteen strapped around him with water also. It belonged to one of the paramilitary organizations of the Party. More than the food, the water was vital as the sun beat down on his body.

A distant noise reached him, that of a motor.

He sat up sharply and looked around. There, on the distance was a boat, coming not directly at him, but at an angle towards him. He almost began to shout and wave at it, but stopped himself short and he laid back down, as low as possible, hoping that he would not be noticed. It had only been this morning that he had swam out, pushing the tires ahead of him before climbing on to be carried away from land by the current. He could not have traveled that far. That boat could simply be a patrol boat and he would be either taken back and shot or the patrol boat would ram his raft and machine gun him in the water, as had happened numerous times to others (such incidents seldom reported in the Western press, which at times seemed sympathetic towards the regime). Since the Communists loudly claimed that they were the people's champions and had bettered the lot of the people, they killed or imprisoned and tortured the people that they caught trying to flee, in a perverted sense of logic that only

they themselves, and their sympathizers understood.

The boat passed by, in the distance.

Before too long, Roberto wished that he *had*
called out to the boat, thought that he must have
traveled far and concluded that it had probably been
an American boat after all.

Later on, that afternoon, as the sun was
setting, he wondered just how much he had
traveled. It was a beautiful sunset, the pinkish sun
almost touching the sea at a distance, suffusing a
reddish glow to the clouds above, in a spectacular
combination of red, blue, pink, orange, yellow and
white.

The sun reached the horizon and slowly
began to descend. There was only the bottom tip
under the horizon. Then, a third of the sun. Its edges
did not seem exactly round now. Half the sun was
gone and now it seemed as if the rest of it was
vanishing faster. Finally, there was just the tip at the
top and then it was gone. A glow was left behind in
the west where it had been, while towards the east
there was dusk. The dusk advanced as the glow
diminished and Roberto began to feel afraid,
although he told himself there was no reason for it.
Nevertheless, his anxiety increased as his own
visibility decreased and his imagination grew in
proportion, so that he began to attribute danger to
the sounds of the waves around him and he began to
imagine that those splashes were the sounds of
carnivorous sea creatures breaking the surface of
the water. Perhaps they were even deep sea
creatures with enormous eyes and oversized fangs,
ready to pull him, and his raft, down into the depths

of the ocean.

Roberto clung tightly to his raft and would dart his head towards the slightest sound and his eyes would strain to make out a shape out of the dark. Occasionally, he thought that he, indeed, saw a rigid fin momentarily break the surface, or the slight blur of a large, fast moving creature going by.

He spent quite some time with these phantoms and it was not until the clouds for the most part went away, that he saw them.

The stars.

The Milky Way.

Thousands, no, millions, no, billions of stars, all over the sky in different degrees of brightness, some slightly bigger than the others, some having an ever so slight color to them. In some parts of the night sky, they were so dense, even though dim, as to seem like an immense mantle. And his fear receded to be replaced by an immense, almost religious, reverence for the sight. Like most people today who are surrounded by city lights, this majestic sight was unknown to him, even though it was a nightly rarity. He was both calmed and awed by the sight.

Presently, the moon appeared over the horizon. Yellow, seemingly bigger than usual, it, too, calmed him further, but in a different manner. This calm was more from seeing an old friend, rather than the calm of being overwhelmed by the majestic splendor of Nature. Even so, the moon revealed itself in such a way as he had never seen it before. It seemed brighter, clearer, warmer, and its brightness greatly illuminated that part of the ocean from where it emerged and spread outward from there. As a result, Roberto saw that the sea around him held no hidden terrors, that everything was as had been in the daytime.

The moon slowly rose into the sky and Roberto, by now quite at peace, took out the impermeable sandwich from his pocket and ate it. He followed it with water from the canteen and was surprised at how thirsty he was. He was even more surprised when he realized that he drained all the water in the canteen. He checked the thermos and made a resolution to ration the remaining water.

If there was rain, he might be able to refill the canteen, he thought.

For a while, he idly watched the mild phosphorescence within the waves and near his makeshift craft.

Eventually, he slept.

He awoke at dawn and stretched, feeling a little stiff. For the most part, he had slept well, all things considered and if one did not count the occasional wave splashing over his head.

There was not much to do, really, just wait and see, and hear. By midmorning, the sun began to bother him a bit, so he again took off his shirt and draped it over his chest and face to keep the sun out. Doing so also gave him a feeling of reassurance by shrinking his world down to the inner tube, wherein he lay.

About an hour later, he heard the faint whir of a motor and he uncovered himself and looked intently towards the direction the noise came from. It was a boat, far away. He tried to stand on the "raft," but fell overboard and had to swim back and climb on. He tried again three times with the same results, so that he ended up kneeling on two tubes, balancing himself by grabbing the canvas with one hand and waving with the other, all the while screaming at the boat in order to get its attention.

The boat went away, oblivious as to his existence.

Disappointed, he laid back down, wondering if that had been his last chance, if he could have done something different, if the people in the boat had seen him at the last moment and were going to return. To shield himself from the sun, he covered up himself again with the shirt.

It was early in the afternoon that things began to take a turn for the worse. There was a different sensation to the raft as it drifted in the current. Roberto looked up from under the shirt and saw, a couple of meters away, one tube apart from the one that he was laying on, with the rope still connecting them, even though in a loose, sagging manner. The other tube had completely drifted away.

Roberto immediately put his shirt on so that it would not be lost and jumped into the water in order to bring the two tires together. He did this with great difficulty, the bobbing tubes bumping against him and having a tendency to drift apart (it had been so much easier in dry land). However, by obtaining the two ends of the rope, climbing back on one of them and pulling with all of his strength, he was able to tie them together again. He looked up at the other one. It was too far away to safely attempt to retrieve it, so he had to be content with two out of three. At least the thermos had not been lost.

It was later on in the afternoon that the young man received his second shock, by witnessing one of those rare manifestations of Nature. It just so happened that most---not all---of the sky had a grayish cloud cover and it was cooler now, whereas the morning had been practically cloud free. Because of this, Roberto did not have his face covered with his shirt, but was wearing it (besides, ever since his raft's breakup he had decided against the practice). As such, he was continually facing up at the sky. As he stared, thinking about this, that and the other, he began to notice that an extension of the cloud seemed to form out of it, downwards, doing so very slowly, very slowly. This extension was somewhat broad, somewhat thin, like an arm. After watching for several minutes it dawned on him what was occurring.

"Rabonube," he gasped, trying to suppress a feeling of panic.

He continued watching it intently, his eyes glued to it, the more so as it was---or appeared to be---directly overhead, but it seemed unable to make up its mind. It would form downwards, stop, change shape and finally reentered the cloud.

Roberto was feeling relieved at this reprieve when he glanced at his right and got the shock of his life. A fully formed "cloudtail," or waterspout, was there at a distance.

How long it had been there he had no idea and no noise was coming from it. It was a thin, very thin half-S-shaped white cloud coming out of a dark flat cloud cover. Where it met the ocean, he could see spray all around it. It was so tall that it touched the sky. It was easily two, three kilometers in length, he thought.

The boy was scared out of his wits, but what could he do? He could not race away, or hide, or swim away. All he could do was watch and watch he did to see if it would come his way. It seemed to be moving so slowly---or was it? Once again, he had no frame of reference. In fact, he was not sure that the funnel was moving at all. It could be stationary for all he knew. One thing that he became certain of after several minutes of watching: it was not coming directly towards him. He reasoned that if it had been, he would not have discerned the half-S-shape, seen from the side, but would have seen, instead, just a long, straight down funnel. As he watched and watched, fascinated, his fear not completely gone, he wondered if the waterspout was sucking up salt water into the cloud. Maybe it would rain saltwater, he wondered. He looked around and noticed that another part of the cloud cover was also trying to form a waterspout. But, unlike the first, it, somehow, seemed unable to do so, it lacked the right conditions and, giving up, went back up into the cloud.

The fully formed waterspout had, in the meantime, traveled a bit, or perhaps the sun now shone though without any cloudy interference in that part of the sky that was not covered by the gray cover. At any rate, there was now a lot of illumination on the side opposite the raft, with the funnel in between. The young man now saw, with fascination, that the center of the funnel was more transparent and clearer than the sides. In fact, he could see turbulence in the center and wondered if it was sea water. He was also struck at how high, how tall, it was and could not help wondering that, if he was sucked up into it, how long would it take him to reach the top---and how long would he stay up before ultimately dropping down to earth (or ocean).

Eventually, the waterspout retracted back into the cloud. Roberto felt that he had been watching for hours. Maybe he had.

For quite some time, the youth kept his eyes peeled for any evidence of more "cloudtails" forming, to the point that he had a few false alarms. Gradually, he began to feel elated. He had been lucky and seen a rare phenomenon. He had also, undeniably, been in danger. This would be some story to tell!

Because of the cloud cover, the sunset was not visible and the transition from daylight to darkness was not as spectacular. In fact, it was rather gloomy.

With darkness, the anxieties from the previous night returned, so that he started at any sudden splashing in the darkness. To be sure, the fears were not as intense as they had been, but they were still present, nonetheless.

Because of the cloud cover, the stars were not visible and could provide no comfort. Neither could the moon.

The boy drew little comfort in the dim luminescence caused by his sweeping his hand in the water.

That night, he hardly slept a wink.

In the morning, the cloud cover was still there, making for a gloomy, yet thankfully cooler day. Even though it was hurricane season, Roberto was not worried. Before he left, there had been no mention at all of any hurricanes forming in the Atlantic or the southern part of the Caribbean, nor had there been any tropical storms that could escalate into a hurricane. A hurricane is one of Nature's minor cataclysms and Roberto had no doubt that he would not survive such an encounter. He had once seen a satellite photograph of a hurricane. The gargantuan whirlpool clouds had completely filled up the Gulf of Mexico. Remembering this photograph suddenly made him feel very small, almost microscopic.

He spent that morning on the lookout for ships with no success.

At one point, a thought occurred to him. Looking around, nothing to see but the sea---no coast, no rocks, no ships, no trees---he frowned. Maybe . . . for all he knew, he could be in the very same spot that he had been when he had begun his journey. Maybe . . . he was really . . . stationary. He brooded over that thought for quite some time.

Around midmorning, he drank some water again from the thermos. It was half full. It was half empty. He was feeling famished, so he took out of his pocket a piece of gristle (a leftover from his sandwich) that was inside the small plastic bag. Out of another pocket, he took out a long piece of string with a hook at the end embedded in a cork. He threw away the cork and the bag, firmly hooked the gristle and let the line overboard. He tied the end of the string to his wrist and waited.

Should he catch something, there was no way to cook it, of course, so he would have to eat it raw. He knew this even though the only thing that he had ever eaten raw had been fruit. But, he had heard that in China and Japan the people there ate raw meat all the time, just like animals, and it was considered normal.

"It all depends on your viewpoint," thought the young man, "and if a Chinaman can do it, well, so can I. Besides, it's better than starving to death."

Anyway, he waited. Maybe he would not catch anything. As he waited for some time for a bite, he noticed one of the many pieces of seaweed that had apparently accompanied him in his voyage. He scooped up the closest one and examined it. For some reason, he noticed the smell of the sea that he had gotten used to by now. The clump of seaweed was the usual brownish-yellow color. It had flat leaves with sharp edges and thick stems. There were little balls attached, which were impossible to pop with his soft, water-wrinkled fingers.

Then, he noticed it, a tiny, tiny crab clinging to its "raft." Because it was of the same color as the seaweed, Roberto had not noticed it at first. He smiled, it was so little that it was cute and he wondered how long it had been traveling. It could have been at sea longer than him, it could have started from the other end of the Caribbean, from Colombia, from all he knew, and so far---it had survived. Its chances for survival were, if anything, much less than his. It being so small, any fish at all, of any size, could make a meal of it, whereas he could make a meal out of most fish. Feeling better on reflecting this, Roberto felt well disposed towards his fellow traveler and gently returned it, with its raft, to the water.

Time passed. He drank some more water. No ships, no planes were seen. Towards midafternoon, he felt a tug at his wrist. The tugging persisted and got stronger and he excitedly pulled the string up. There was something definitely caught. A black fish slowly became visible. A grouper!

186

Now that he had the fish in front of him, looking at him, the idea of eating it raw became repulsive. What to do with it?

He looked at it. The hook was lodged firmly deep in its throat. It could not possibly escape, so he simply tied it to his raft and, with a few feet of slack, threw it overboard. That way it would stay alive and fresh until his hunger would overcome his squeamishness. The grouper struggled for a while, then ultimately stopped doing so, exhausted.

That decision turned out to be a mistake.

Before an hour had passed, the boy felt a shudder. He looked around agitatedly and saw shark fins where the grouper should be. Roberto quickly pulled the string in, though with difficulty, and saw that there were two small sharks involved. Pulling the last of the string, he withdrew the tattered meager remains of the grouper. There was not much left, but at least it would serve as bait, later on.

The raft shuddered again and Roberto realized that a shark must have scraped against it. He quickly drew in his legs, which he had been stupidly dangling in the water.

There were at least two of them and the youth could not keep track of their movements. The raft shuddered again, this time more fiercely and he realized with horror that a shark was actually taking a bite out of the canvas.

Did sharks *eat* canvas?

It swam off, apparently unimpressed. He saw a small, white object in the canvas at water's edge and, making sure that there were no sharks around, he reached over and pulled at it. It was a sharp, serrated, triangular tooth.

The sharks did not return, but the young man waited a long time before relaxing enough to extend his limbs.

And the thermos was gone.

The night was miserable. Roberto was flipped over more than once and had to climb back on his threadbare raft. Additionally, his previous terrors of sightless noises had a more tangible basis: the sharks could return.

The clouds were gone by morning and the young man was once again treated to a colorful sunrise. He was unable to appreciate it as much as he had in the past because of his exhaustion.

He kept a lookout for ships that morning, but none were visible and the monotony was oppressive. Ocean and waves. Ocean and waves. Ocean and waves. Ocean and waves.

He was also famished and dehydrated.

By noon, the sun was quite an irritant and he draped part of the overhanging canvas over his face and chest. Almost immediately, without intending to, he fell asleep and slept soundly.

He had slept for some time, he knew that, and he had been hearing it for some time, when the sound broke through some psychological threshold and woke him up. It was a ship's motor. Nearby, he jerked off the shirt and there, just a couple of dozen meters away was a large ship! He sat up, screaming and waving. He could see figures on the ship. They waved back! They saw him!

Slowly, the ship ponderously moved towards him, very slowly. He was scooped up by a number of hands and half a dozen voices in an unknown language assailed him.

"Chi e?" said one.

"E un uomo," said another.

"Uomo? E un bambino!" another answered back, grinning.

"Senta, di dove e lei?" one addressed him.

"Senta, bambino. Parla Italiano? Parla Italiano?" another asked him.

Roberto shook his head.

"No, no soy Italiano," he answered.

"Parla inglese? Parla francese? Espagnol?"

"Soy de Cuba," said Roberto, telling them where he was from. *"De Cuba. Hablo Español. Ustedes son Italiano?"*

"A! Di Cuba. E di Cuba," said one.

"Un Cubano! Un pazzo Cubano," said another, grinning.

"Si. Siamo Italiano."

"Ah, Cuba! Fidel Castro, il gran bufone. Lui e di Cuba. Io di credo che lui voglie andare a America. A Miami."

"Si! Yo quiero ir a Miami! Y Ustedes. . . .?" Roberto motioned to them, *"van a Miami?"*

"Si!" one of them responded. *"Andiamoci a Miami, no a Cuba. Non avete paura,"* he said nodding and reassuring him with his hand.

Roberto felt weak.

"Agua por favor," he pleaded; they immediately understood and gave him a glassful of water. He gulped it down in a flash and another and another and another in front of their astounded faces.

He felt better, now. He had made it.

He was now safe.

He felt big.

Free.

COCKFIGHTS

We were watching the local news on the TV, my wife and I. One particular story caught her attention. It was a report about the police having broken up a cockfight on the outskirts of town and arrested the men responsible.

"That's terrible," she remarked.

"What?"

"Making those birds fight, and gambling on them."

"Why?"

"It's just wrong."

"Cockfighting is very common throughout the world. And in the Orient, they even have fights between Siamese Fighting Fish."

"I don't care. Making animals suffer is wrong."

There was a pause in our conversation.

"I used to be involved in cockfights," I volunteered.

"You were?"

"Yep. As a kid in Cuba. It used to be very common. Even in nice, middle class neighborhoods in the capital. The kids used to keep the roosters in the back yard, or in cages in the garages."

"How many did you have?"

"Oh, just one. Each kid would have just one"

"So it was the kids that did it?"

"Sure! Mind you, many of the men also bet on their cockfights, but this was like a game of baseball in the neighborhood."

"Did they fight to the death?"

"Oh, no! As soon as one won the fight, it'd

come to an end. It really wasn't as gruesome as you think it is. Now, I don't know about the cockfights with the adults, if they were to the death or not, probably not."

"So did yours win any fights?"

"Yeah, it won some, it lost some. I was fond of that rooster."

"What happened to it?"

"Well, after the Communists took over the country, cockfighting pretty much disappeared."

"Oh, did they abolish cockfighting?"

"No, after the Communists took over the country there was very little to eat, so we ate the roosters."

www.ingramcontent.com/pod-product-compliance
Lightning Source LLC
Chambersburg PA
CBHW021000180626
46814CB00003B/1178